"I Know Your Type, O'Riley," Amanda Said.

Sloan rocked back on his heels. "Do you?"

Amanda fought to push her arms through the sleeves of her wrap. "You swagger from town to town and fill a few free hours with a quick roll between the sheets with any available woman." She pulled the tie on the wrap tight. "Well, I'm not available."

"You figure you got me pegged, huh?" He didn't touch her, but the look in his eyes was enough to have her bracing. "You can take this as a warning, Calhoun. This isn't finished between us. I'm going to have you."

"*Have* me?" She took one long step toward him. "Why, you conceited—"

"You can save the flattery for later. There *will* be a later, Amanda, when it's just you and me. And I promise you, it won't be quick." He smiled. "When I make love with you, I'm going to take my time." He ran a finger down the collar of her wrap. "And I'm going to drive you crazy."

Dear Reader:

Happy summertime reading from everyone here! July is an extra-special month, because Nora Roberts—at long last—has written a much-anticipated Silhouette Desire. It's called *A Man for Amanda* and it's part of her terrific series, THE CALHOUN WOMEN. Look for the distinctive portrait of Amanda Calhoun on the cover.

And also look for the portrait of July's *Man of the Month,* Niall Rankin, on the cover of Kathleen Creighton's *In From the Cold*. Ms. Creighton has written a number of books for Silhouette Intimate Moments. Please *don't* miss this story; I know you'll love it!

There is something for everyone this month—sensuous, emotional romances written just for *you!* July is completed with other must-reads from the talented pens of your *very* favorites: Helen R. Myers, Barbara Boswell, Joan Johnston and Linda Turner. So enjoy, enjoy....

All the best,

Lucia Macro
Senior Editor

NORA ROBERTS

A MAN FOR AMANDA

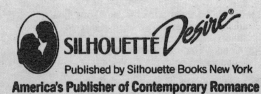

SILHOUETTE *Desire*®

Published by Silhouette Books New York

America's Publisher of Contemporary Romance

To Joyce,
from one baby sister to another

SILHOUETTE BOOKS
300 East 42nd St., New York, N.Y. 10017

A MAN FOR AMANDA

ISBN: 0-373-05649-4

First Silhouette Books printing July 1991

Books by Nora Roberts

Silhouette Romance

Irish Thoroughbred #81
Blithe Images #127
Song of the West #143
Search for Love #163
Island of Flowers #180
From This Day #199
Her Mother's Keeper #215
Untamed #252
Storm Warning #274
Sullivan's Woman #280
Less of a Stranger #299
Temptation #529
‡*Courting Catherine* #801

Silhouette Special Edition

The Heart's Victory #59
Reflections #100
Dance of Dreams #116
First Impressions #162
The Law Is a Lady #175
Opposites Attract #199
*Playing the Odds #225
*Tempting Fate #235
**All the Possibilities* #247
**One Man's Art* #259
Summer Desserts #271
Second Nature #288
One Summer #306
Lessons Learned #318
A Will and a Way #345
**For Now, Forever* #361
Local Hero #427
°*The Last Honest Woman* #451
°*Dance to the Piper* #463
°*Skin Deep* #475
Loving Jack #499
Best Laid Plans #511
The Welcoming #553
Taming Natasha #583
°*Without a Trace* #625

Silhouette Intimate Moments

Once More with Feeling #2
Tonight and Always #12
This Magic Moment #25
Endings and Beginnings #33
A Matter of Choice #49
Rules of the Game #70
The Right Path #85
Partners #94
Boundary Lines #114
Dual Image #123
The Art of Deception #131
†*Affaire Royale* #142
Treasures Lost, Treasures Found #150
Risky Business #160
Mind Over Matter #185
†*Command Performance* #198
†*The Playboy Prince* #212
Irish Rose #232
·*The Name of the Game* #264
Gabriel's Angel #300
Time Was #313
Times Change #317
Night Shift #365
Night Shadow #373

Silhouette Desire

‡*A Man for Amanda* #649

Silhouette Books

Silhouette Christmas Stories 1986
"Home for Christmas"
Silhouette Summer Sizzlers 1989
"Impulse"

‡The Calhoun Women

*MacGregor Series

°The O'Hurleys!

†Cordina's Royal Family

THE CALHOUN WOMEN

Fergus Calhoun
m.
Bianca Halloran

Colleen

Ethan
m.
Lillian Scott

Sean

Judson
m.
Deliah Brady

Cordelia
m.
Arthur McPike

Suzanna
Suzanna's Surrender
Silhouette Intimate Moments #397
September 1991
m.
Baxter Dumont (d)

Alex   Jenny

Lilah
For the Love of Lilah
Silhouette Special Edition #685
August 1991

Amanda
A Man for Amanda
Silhouette Desire #649
July 1991
m.
Sloan O'Riley

Catherine
Courting Catherine
Silhouette Romance #801
June 1991
m.
Trenton St. James III

Prologue

Bar Harbor
June 8, 1913

In the afternoon, I walked to the cliffs. The day, our first day back in The Towers, was bright and warm. The rumble of the sea was as I had left it ten long months ago. There was a fishing boat chugging over the blue-green water, and a neat sloop gliding cheerfully along. So much was the same, and yet, one vital change dimmed the day for me.

He was not there.

It was wrong of me to wish to find him waiting where I had left him so many months ago. To find him painting as he always did, slicing the brush against canvas like a dueler in the heat of battle. It was wrong of me to wish to see him turn, look at me with those intense gray eyes—to see him smile, to hear him say my name.

Yet I did wish it.

My heart was dancing in my breast as I rushed from the house to race across the lawn, past the gardens and down the slope.

The cliffs were there, so high and proud, jutting up to the pure summer sky. The sea, almost calm today, mirrored the color so that it seemed I stood cupped in a lovely blue ball. The rocks tumbled down before me, down and down to where the waves slapped and hissed. Behind me, the towers of my summer home, my husband's home, speared up, arrogant and beautiful.

How strange that I should love the house when I have known such unhappiness inside it.

I reminded myself that I am Bianca Calhoun, wife of Fergus Calhoun, mother to Colleen and Ethan and Sean. I am a respected woman, a dutiful wife, a devoted mother. My marriage is not a warm one, but that does not alter the vows I took. There is no place in my life for romantic fancies and sinful dreams.

Still, I stood and I waited. But he did not come. Christian, the lover I have taken only with my heart, did not come. He may not even be on the island any longer. Perhaps he has packed up his canvases and brushes, moved from his cottage and gone on to paint some other sea, some other sky.

It would be best. I know it would be best. Since I met him last summer, I have hardly gone an hour without thinking of him. Yet I have a husband I respect, three children I love more than my life. It is to them I must be faithful, not to the memory of something that never was. And never could be.

The sun is setting as I sit and write by the window of my tower. In a short time I must go down and help Nanny put my babies to bed. Little Sean has grown so, and is already beginning to toddle. Soon he will be as quick as Ethan. Colleen, quite the young lady at four, wants a new pink dress.

It is of them I must think, my children, my precious loves, and not of Christian.

It will be a quiet night, one of very few we will have during our summer on Mount Desert Island. Fergus has already talked of giving a dinner dance next week. I must . . .

He is there. Down below on the cliffs. He is hardly more than a shadow with the distance and the dimming light. Yet I know it is he. Just as I knew, as I stood and pressed my hand to the glass, that he was looking up, looking for me. However impossible it is, I would swear I could hear him call my name. So softly.

Bianca.

One

———

He was a solid wall of denim and muscle. Ramming into him knocked the wind out of her lungs and the packages out of her hands. In her rush to get from one place to the next, she didn't even bother to glance at him but dove to save the flying boxes.

If he'd been looking where he'd been going, she wouldn't have run into him. Amanda managed to bite her tongue before she snapped out the thought, and scowled instead at the run-down heels of his boots. In a hurry, as usual, she knelt on the sidewalk outside the boutique where she'd been shopping, to gather up her scattered packages.

"Let me give you a hand, honey."

The slow southwestern drawl grated on her nerves. She had a million things to do, and scrambling on the sidewalk with a tourist wasn't on her schedule. "I've got it," she muttered, leaning over so that her chin-length hair drifted down to curtain her face. Everything was grating on her nerves today, she thought as she hurried to restack bags and boxes. This little irritation was the last in a long line.

"It's an awful lot for one person to carry."

"I can manage, thanks." She reached for a box just as her persistent helper did the same. The brief tug-of-war had the top slipping off and the contents spilling onto the sidewalk.

"Now, that's mighty pretty." There was amused, masculine approval in the voice as he scooped up a scrap of thin red silk that pretended to be a nightie.

Amanda snatched it from him and stuffed it into one of the bags. "Do you mind?"

"No, ma'am. I sure don't."

Amanda pushed back her tumbled hair and took her first good look at him. So far, all she'd seen were a pair of cowboy boots and the line of faded denim from knee to ankle. There was a great deal more of him. Even crouched down beside her he looked big. Shoulders, hands. Mouth, she thought nastily. Right now he was using it to grin at her. It might, under different circumstances, have been an engaging enough grin. But at the moment it was stuck in the middle of a face she'd decided to dislike on sight.

Not that it wasn't a good one, with its slashing warrior's cheekbones, velvet green eyes and deep tan. The curl of his reddish-blond hair over the collar of his denim shirt might have been charming. If he hadn't been in her way.

"I'm in a hurry," she told him.

"I noticed." He flipped a long finger through her hair to tuck it behind her ear. "Looked like you were on the way to a fire when you plowed into me."

"If you'd moved," she began, then shook her head. Arguing would take time she simply didn't have. "Never mind." Grabbing at packages, she rose. "Excuse me."

"Hold on."

He unfolded himself as she tapped her foot and waited. Disconcerted, she frowned up at him. At five feet ten inches, she was accustomed to meeting most men almost eye to eye. With this one she had several extra inches to go. "What?"

"I can give you a ride to that fire if you need it."

Her brow arched in her frostiest look. "That won't be necessary."

Using a fingertip, he pushed a box back in place before it could slide out of her grip. "You look like you could use a little help."

"I'm perfectly capable of getting where I'm going, thank you."

He didn't doubt it for a minute. "Then maybe you can help me." He liked the way her hair kept falling into her eyes, and the impatient way she kept blowing it away again. "I just got into town this morning." His gaze lazily skimmed her face. "I thought maybe you could make some suggestions about...what I should do with myself."

At the moment, she had a pocketful of them. "Try the chamber of commerce." She started by him, then whirled when his hand came down on her arm. "Look, buster, I don't know how they do things back in Tucson—"

"Oklahoma City," he corrected.

"Wherever, but around here, cops take a dim view of men who hassle women on the streets."

"That so?"

"You bet it's so."

"Well then, I'll have to watch my step since I plan to be around awhile."

"I'll hang out a bulletin. Now, excuse me."

"Just one more thing." He held up a pair of brief black panties embroidered with red roses. "I think you forgot this."

She grabbed the bikinis, then stalked off as she balled them into her pocket.

"Nice meeting you," he called after her, and laughed when she doubled her already hurried pace.

Twenty minutes later, Amanda gathered up her packages from the back seat of her car. Balancing some under her chin, she kicked the door closed with her foot. She'd nearly forgotten about the encounter already. There was too much on her mind. Behind her, the house rose up into the sky, its gray stones staid, its towers and peaks fanciful and its porches sagging. Next to her family, there was nothing Amanda loved more than The Towers.

She raced up the steps, avoided a rotting board then struggled to free a hand enough to open the towering front door. "Aunt Coco!" The moment she stepped into the hall, an oversize black puppy raced down the stairs. On the third from the bottom, he tripped, rolled and went sprawling onto the gleaming chestnut floor. "Almost made it that time, Fred."

Pleased with himself, Fred danced around Amanda's legs as she continued to call for her aunt.

"Coming. I'm coming." Tall and stately, Cordelia Calhoun McPike hurried in from the rear of the house. She wore peach linen slacks under a splattered white apron. "I was in the kitchen. We're going to try my new recipe for cannelloni tonight."

"Is C.C. home?"

"Oh, no, dear." Coco patted the hair she'd tinted the day before to Moonlit Blonde. In an old habit, she peeked into the hall mirror to make certain the shade suited her—for the moment. "She's down at her garage. Something about rocker arms, I think—though what rocking chairs have to do with cars and engines, I can't say."

"Great. Come upstairs, I want to show you what I got."

"Looks like you bought out the shops. Here, let me help you." Coco managed to grab two bags before Amanda dashed up the stairs.

"I had the best time."

"But you hate to shop."

"For myself. This was different. Still, everything took longer than I thought it would, so I was afraid I wouldn't get back and be able to stash it all before C.C. got home." She rushed into her room to dump everything onto the big four-poster bed. "Then this stupid man got in my way and knocked everything all over the sidewalk." Amanda stripped off her jacket, folded it, then laid it neatly over the back of a chair. "Then he had the nerve to try to pick me up."

"Really?" Always interested in liaisons, romances and assignations, Coco tilted her head. "Was he attractive?"

"If you go for the Wild Bill Hickok type. Anyway, I made it—no thanks to him."

As Amanda sorted through the bags, Fred tried twice, unsuccessfully, to leap onto the bed. He ended by sitting on the rug to watch.

"I found some wonderful decorations for the bridal shower." She began to pull out white-and-silver bells, crepe paper swans, balloons. "I love this frilly parasol," she went on. "Not C.C.'s style maybe, but I thought if we hung it up over...Aunt Coco." With a sigh, Amanda sat on the bed. "Don't start crying again."

"I can't help it." Already sniffling, Coco took an embroidered hankie from her apron pocket and dabbed carefully at her eyes. "She's the baby, after all. The youngest of my four little girls."

"There's not one of the Calhoun women who could be called little," Amanda pointed out.

"You're still my babies, and have been ever since your mother and father died." Coco used the hankie expertly. She didn't want to smear her mascara. "Every time I think of her being married—and in only a matter of days, really—I just fill up. I adore Trenton, you know." Thinking of her future nephew, she blew delicately into the hankie. "He's a wonderful man, and I knew they'd be perfect together right from the start, but it's all so fast."

"You're telling me." Amanda combed a hand through her sleek cap of hair. "I've barely had time to organize. How anyone expects to put on a wedding with barely three weeks notice—or why they'd want to try—is beyond me. They'd be better off eloping."

"Don't say that." Scandalized, Coco stuck her hankie back into her pocket. "Why, I'd be furious if they cheated me out of this wedding. And if you think you can when your time comes, think again."

"My time isn't going to come for years, if ever." Meticulously Amanda tidied the decorations again.

"Men are as far down on my list of priorities as they can get."

"You and your lists." Coco clucked her tongue. "Let me tell you, Mandy, the one thing you can't plan in this life is falling in love. Your sister certainly didn't plan it, and look at her. Squeezing fittings for a wedding dress in between her carburetors and transmissions. Your time may come sooner than you think. Why just this morning when I was reading my tea leaves—"

"Oh, Aunt Coco, not the tea leaves."

Grandly Coco drew herself up to her considerable height. "I've read some very fascinating things in the tea leaves. After our last séance, I'd think you'd be a bit less cynical."

"Maybe something happened at the séance, but—"

"Maybe?"

"All right, something did happen." Letting out a deep breath, Amanda shrugged. "I know C.C. got an image—"

"A vision."

"Whatever—of Great-Grandmama Bianca's emerald necklace." And it had been spooky, she admitted to herself, the way C.C. had been able to describe it, though no one had seen the two tiers of emeralds and diamonds in decades. "And no one who's lived in this house could deny that they've felt some—some presence or something up in Bianca's tower."

"Aha!"

"But that doesn't mean I'm going to start gazing into crystal balls."

"You're just too literal minded, Mandy. I can't think where you get it from. Perhaps from my Aunt Colleen. Fred, we must not chew on the Irish lace," Coco cautioned as Fred began to gnaw on Amanda's bed-spread. "In any case, we were speaking of tea leaves. When I took a reading this morning, I saw a man."

Amanda rose to hide the decorations in her closet. "You saw a man in your teacup."

"You know very well it doesn't work precisely like that. I saw a man, and I had the strongest feeling that he's very close."

"Maybe it's the plumber. He's been underfoot for days."

"No, it's not the plumber. This man—he's close, but he's not from the island." She let her eyes unfocus as she did when she practiced looking psychic. "In fact he's from some distance away. He's going to be an important part of our lives. And—I'm quite sure of this—he's going to be vitally important to one of you girls."

"Lilah can have him," Amanda decided, thinking of her free-spirited older sister. "Where is she anyway?"

"Oh, she was meeting someone after work. Rod or Tod or Dominick."

"Damn it." Amanda scooped up her jacket to hang it neatly in the closet. "We were supposed to go through more of the papers. She knew I was counting on her. We have to find some lead as to where the emeralds are hidden."

"We'll find them, dear." Distracted, Coco poked through the other packages. "When the time is right. Bianca wants us to. I believe she'll show us the next step very soon."

"We need more than blind faith and mystic visions. Bianca could have hidden them anywhere." Scowling, she plopped down onto the bed again.

She didn't care about the money—though the Calhoun emeralds were reputed to be worth a fortune. It was the publicity that had resulted when Trent, her sister's fiancé, had contracted to buy The Towers, and the old legend had become public knowledge. Amanda's idea of an ordered existence had been thrown into chaos since the first story had hit.

It certainly made good print, Amanda mused as her aunt oohed and aahed over the lingerie she had bought for her sister's shower.

Early in the second decade of the century, when the resort of Bar Harbor was in its elegant heyday, Fergus Calhoun had built The Towers as an opulent summer home. There on the cliffs overlooking Frenchman Bay, he and his wife, Bianca, and their three children had vacationed, giving elaborate parties for other members of the well-heeled society.

And there, Bianca had met a young artist. They had fallen in love. It was said that Bianca had been torn between duty and her heart. Her marriage, which had been firmly supported by her parents, had been a cold one. With her heart leading her, she had planned to leave her husband and had packed away a treasure box that had contained the emeralds Fergus had given her on the birth of their second child and first son. The whereabouts of the necklace was a mystery as, according to legend, she had thrown herself from the tower window, overwhelmed with guilt and despair.

Now, eighty years later, interest in the necklace had been revived. Even as the remaining Calhouns searched through decades of papers and ledgers for a clue, reporters and hopeful fortune hunters had become a daily nuisance.

Amanda took it personally. The legend, and the people in it, belonged to her family. The sooner the necklace was located, the better. Once a mystery was solved, interest faded quickly.

"When is Trent coming back?" she asked her aunt.

"Soon." Sighing, Coco stroked the silky red chemise. "As soon as he ties things up in Boston, he'll be on his way. He can't stand being away from C.C. There will barely be enough time to begin the renovations on the west wing before they'll be off on their honeymoon." Tears filled her eyes again. "Their honeymoon."

"Don't start, Aunt Coco. Think of what a fabulous job you'll do catering the reception. It's going to be great practice for you. This time next year you'll be starting your new career as chef for The Towers Retreat, the most intimate of the St. James hotels."

"Imagine it." Coco patted her hand at her breast.

At the knock on the front door, Fred was up and howling.

"You stay here and imagine it, Aunt Coco. I'll go answer the door."

In a race with Fred, she clattered down the steps. When the dog's four legs tangled, sending him somersaulting, she laughed and gathered him up. She was snuggling the dog against her cheek when she opened the door.

"You!"

The tone of her voice had Fred quaking. Not so the man who stood at the threshold, grinning at her. "Small world," he said in the same slow drawl he'd used when they'd knelt on the sidewalk. "I'm liking it better all the time."

"You followed me."

"No, ma'am. Though it would've been a damn good idea. The name's O'Riley. Sloan O'Riley."

"I don't care what your name is, you can turn around and start walking." She started to slam the door in his face, but he slapped a hand against it and held it wide.

"I don't think that's such a good idea. I've come a long way to get a look at the house."

Her dark blue eyes narrowed. "Oh, have you? Well, let me tell you something, this is a home, a private home. I don't care what you've read in the papers and how badly you want a shot at looking under loose stones for the emeralds. This isn't Treasure Island, and I've had my fill of people like you who think they can just come knocking at the door, or sneaking into the garden at night with a pick and shovel."

She looked just fine, Sloan thought as he waited out the tirade. Every furious inch of her. She was tall for a woman and lean with it—but not too lean. She curved out nicely in all the right places. She looked as though she could ride hard all day and still have the energy to kick up her heels at night. Stubborn chin, he decided, and approved. When she jutted it out, her warm brown hair swayed with the movement. Big blue eyes. Even while they spit fire they reminded him of cornflowers. When it wasn't scowling or swearing, he imagined her full, shapely mouth would be soft.

Soft and tasty.

"You run down yet?" he asked when she stopped to take a breath.

"No, and if you don't leave right now, I'm going to let my dog loose on you."

Taking his cue, Fred leaped out of her arms. With neck fur bristling, he bared his teeth in a growl.

"Looks pretty fierce," Sloan commented, then hunkered down to hold out the back of his hand. Fred sniffed it, then his tail began to wag joyously as Sloan scratched his ears. "Yep, pretty fierce animal you got here."

"That's it." Amanda set her hands on her hips. "I'm getting the gun."

Before she could turn inside to look for the fictitious weapon, Coco came downstairs.

"Who is it, Amanda?"

"Dead meat."

"I beg your pardon?" She stepped up to the door. The moment she spotted Sloan her ingrained vanity took over. In the blink of an eye she whipped her apron off. "Hello." Her smile was warm and feminine as she extended a hand. "I'm Cordelia McPike."

"A pleasure, ma'am." Sloan brought her fingertips to his mouth. "As I was just telling your sister here—"

"Oh, my." Coco let out a trill of delighted laughter. "Amanda's not my sister. She's my niece. The third daughter of my late brother—my much older brother."

"My mistake."

"Aunt Coco, this jerk knocked me down outside of the boutique, then followed me home. He just wants to wheedle his way into the house because of the necklace."

"Now, Mandy, you mustn't be so harsh."

"That's partially true, Mrs. McPike." Sloan gave Amanda a slow nod. "Your niece and I did have a run-in. Guess I didn't get out of her way in time. And I am trying to get into the house."

"I see." Torn between hope and doubt, Coco sighed. "I'm terribly sorry, but I don't think it would be possible to let you in. You see we have so much to do with the wedding—"

Sloan's eyes whipped back to Amanda. "You getting married?"

"My sister," she said tightly. "Not that it's any of your business. Now if you'll excuse us?"

"I wouldn't want to intrude, so I'll just be on my way. If you'll tell Trent that O'Riley was by, I'd appreciate it."

"O'Riley?" Coco repeated, then fluttered her hands. "Goodness, are you Mr. O'Riley? Please come in. Oh, I do apologize."

"Aunt Coco—"

"This is Mr. O'Riley, Amanda."

"I realize that. Why the devil have you let him in the house?"

"*The* Mr. O'Riley," Coco continued. "The one Trenton called about this morning. Don't you remember—of course you don't remember, because I didn't tell you." She patted her hands to her cheeks. "I'm afraid I'm just so flustered after keeping you standing outside that way."

"Don't you worry about it," he said to Coco. "It's an honest mistake."

"Aunt Coco." Amanda stood with her hand on the doorknob, ready to pitch the intruder out bodily if necessary. "Who is this O'Riley and why did Trent tell you to expect him?"

"Mr. O'Riley's the architect," Coco said, beaming.

Eyes narrowing, Amanda studied him from the tip of his boots to his wavy, disordered hair. "This is an architect?"

"Our architect. Mr. O'Riley will be in charge of the renovations for the retreat, and our living quarters. We'll all be working with Mr. O'Riley—"

"Sloan," he said.

"Sloan." Coco fluttered her lashes. "For quite some time."

"Terrific." Amanda let the door slam.

Sloan hooked his thumbs in his jean pockets and gave her a slow smile. "My thoughts exactly."

Two

"Where are our manners?" Coco said. "Here we are keeping you standing in the hall. Please, come in and sit down. What can I offer you? Coffee, tea?"

"Beer in a long-necked bottle," Amanda muttered.

Sloan merely smiled at her. "There you go."

"Beer?" Coco ushered him into the parlor, wishing she'd had a moment to freshen the flowers in the vase and plump the pillows. "I have some very nice beer in the kitchen that I use for my spiced shrimp. Amanda, you'll entertain Sloan, won't you?"

"Sure. Why not?" Though she wasn't feeling particularly gracious, Amanda gestured to a chair, then took one across from him in front of the fireplace. "I suppose I should apologize."

Sloan reached down to pet Fred, who had followed them in. "What for?"

"I wouldn't have been so rude if I'd realized why you were here."

"Is that so?" As Fred settled down on the rug between them, Sloan eased back in his chair to study his unwilling hostess.

After a humming ten seconds, she struggled not to fidget. "It was a natural enough mistake."

"If you say so. What exactly are these emeralds you figured I was here to dig up?"

"The Calhoun emeralds." When he only lifted a brow, she shook her head. "My great-grandmother's emerald necklace. It's been in all the papers."

"I haven't had much time to read the papers. I've been in Budapest." He reached into his pocket and pulled out a long, slim cigar. "Mind?"

"Go ahead." Automatically she rose to fetch an ashtray from across the room. Sloan considered it a pleasure to watch that out-of-my-way walk of hers. "I'm surprised Trent didn't mention it."

Sloan struck a match and took his sweet time lighting the cigar. He took an appreciative drag, then blew out a lazy stream of smoke. All the while, he was taking stock of the room, with its sagging sofa, the glistening Baccarat, the elegant old wainscoting and the peeling paint.

"I got a cable from Trent telling me about the house and his plans, and asking me to take it on."

"You agreed to take a job like this without even seeing the property first?"

"Seemed like the thing to do at the time." She sure had pretty eyes, Sloan thought. Suspicious, but pretty. He wondered how they'd look if he ever managed to get a smile out of her. "Besides, Trent wouldn't have asked if he didn't think I'd get a kick out of it."

Her foot began to tap as it did when she had sat in one place too long. "You know Trent well then?"

"We go back a few years. We were at Harvard together."

"Harvard?" Her foot stopped tapping as she gaped at him. "You went to Harvard?"

Another man might have been insulted. Sloan was amused. "Why, shucks, ma'am," he murmured, exaggerating his drawl, then watching her cheeks flush.

"I didn't mean to . . . it's just that you don't really seem—"

"The Ivy League type?" he suggested before he took another pull on the cigar. "Guess appearances can be deceiving. Take the house here for instance."

"The house?"

"You take your first look at it from the outside and it's hard to figure if it's supposed to be a fortress, a castle or an architect's nightmare. But you take the time to look again, and you see it's not supposed to be anything but what it is. A timeless piece of work, on the arrogant side, strong, maybe stubborn enough to hold its own, but with just enough fancy to add some charm." He grinned at her. "Some people believe that a house reflects the personality of the people who live in it."

He rose when Coco came back in wheeling a tray. "Oh, sit down, please. It's such a treat to have a man in the house. Isn't it, Mandy?"

"I'm all aflutter."

"I hope the beer's all right." She lifted a brimming pilsner glass from the tray.

"I'm sure it's fine."

"Do try some of these canapés. Mandy, I've brought us some wine." Delighted with the chance to socialize, she smiled at Sloan over the rim of her glass. "Has Amanda been telling you about the house?"

"We were just getting to it." Sloan took a long swallow of beer. "Trent wrote that it's been in the family since the early part of the century."

"Oh, yes. With Suzanna's children—Suzanna's my eldest niece—we've had five generations of Calhouns at The Towers. Fergus—" she gestured to the portrait of a dour-faced man over the mantel "—my grandfather, built The Towers in 1904, as a summer home. He and his wife, Bianca, had three children before she threw herself out of the tower window." As always, the idea of dying for love had her sighing. "I don't believe Grandpapa was ever quite right after that. He went insane later in life, but we kept him in a very nice institution."

"Aunt Coco, I'm sure Mr. O'Riley isn't interested in the family history."

"Not interested," Sloan agreed as he tapped out his cigar. "Fascinated. Don't stop now, Mrs. McPike."

"Oh, call me Coco. Everyone does." She fluffed her hair. "The house passed along to my father, Ethan. He was their second child, but the first son. Grandpapa was very adamant about the Calhoun line. His— Ethan's—elder sister, Colleen, was miffed about the arrangement. She rarely speaks to any of us to this day."

"For which we're all eternally grateful," Amanda put in.

"Well, yes. She can be a bit—overwhelming. That left Uncle Sean, my father's younger brother. He had a spot of trouble with a woman and sailed off to the West Indies before I was born. When my father was killed, the house passed to my brother, Judson. After his marriage he and his wife decided to live here year-round. They adored the place.'' She glanced around the parlor with its cracked walls and faded curtains. ''Judson had wonderful plans for revamping the house, but tragically he and Deliah were killed before he could begin to implement them. Then I came here to care for Amanda and her three sisters. Have another canapé.''

''Thanks. Can I ask why you decided to convert part of your home into a hotel?''

''That was Trent's idea. We're all so grateful to him, aren't we, Amanda?''

Since she accepted the fact that there would be no winding down Aunt Coco, Amanda smiled. ''Yes, we are.''

Coco sipped delicately from her glass. ''To be frank, we were in some financial distress. Do you believe in fate, Sloan?''

''I'm Irish and Cherokee.'' He spread his long fingers. ''That doesn't give me any other choice.''

''Well then, you'll understand. It was fated that Trent's father would see The Towers while he was sailing in Frenchman Bay, and seeing it, develop a deep desire for it. When the St. James's corporation offered to buy the house and turn it into a resort hotel, we were torn. It was our home after all, the only home my girls have ever known, but the upkeep...''

''I understand.''

''Things happen for the best,'' Coco put in. ''And it was really very exciting and romantic. We were on the brink, the very brink, of being forced to sell, when Trent fell in love with C.C. Of course he understood how much the house meant to her, and came up with this marvelous plan of converting the west wing into hotel suites. That way we can keep the house, and overcome the financial difficulty of maintaining it."

"Everyone gets what they want," Sloan agreed.

"Exactly." Coco leaned forward. "With your heritage, I imagine you also believe in spirits."

"Aunt Coco—"

"Now, Mandy, I know how practical minded you are. It baffles me," she said to Sloan. "All that Celtic blood and not a mystical bone in her body."

Amanda gestured with her glass. "I leave that for you and Lilah."

"Lilah's my other niece," Coco told Sloan. "She's very fey. But we were talking about the supernatural. Do you have an opinion?"

Sloan set his glass aside. "I don't think you could have a house like this without a ghost or two."

"There." Coco clapped her hands together. "I knew as soon as I saw you we'd be kindred spirits. Bianca's still here, you see. Why at our last séance I felt her so strongly." She ignored Amanda's groan. "C.C. did, too, and she's nearly as practical minded as Amanda. Bianca wants us to find the necklace."

"The Calhoun emeralds?" Sloan asked.

"Yes. We've been searching for clues, but the clutter of eight decades is daunting. And the publicity has been a bother."

"That's a mild word for it." Amanda scowled into her glass.

"It might turn up during the renovation," Sloan suggested.

"We're hoping." Coco tapped one carefully manicured finger against her lips. "I think another séance might be in order. I'm sure you're very sensitive."

Amanda choked on her wine. "Aunt Coco, Mr. O'Riley has come here to work, not to play ghosts and goblins."

"I like mixing business and pleasure." He toasted Amanda with his glass. "In fact, I make a habit of it."

A new thought jumped into Coco's mind. "You're not from the island, Sloan."

"No, Oklahoma."

"Really? That's quite a distance." She slid her gaze smugly toward Amanda. "As architect for the renovations, you'll be very important to all of us."

"I'd like to think so," he said, baffled by the arched look Coco sent her niece.

"Tea leaves," Coco murmured, then rose. "I must go check on dinner. You will join us, won't you?"

He'd planned on taking a quick look at the house then going back to the hotel to sleep for ten hours. The annoyed look on Amanda's face changed his mind. An evening with her might be a better cure for jet lag. "I'd be mighty pleased to."

"Wonderful. Mandy, why don't you show Sloan the west wing while I finish things up?"

"Tea leaves?" Sloan asked when Coco glided from the room.

"You're better off in the dark." Resigned, she rose and gestured to the doorway. "Shall we get started?"

"That's a fine idea." He followed her into the hall and up the curving staircase. "Which do you like, Amanda or Mandy?"

She shrugged. "I answer to either."

"Different images. Amanda's cool and composed. Mandy's…softer." She smelled cool, he thought. Like a quiet breeze on a hot, dusty day.

At the top of the stairs she stopped to face him. "What kind of image is Sloan?"

He stayed one step below her so that they were eye to eye. Instinct told him they'd both prefer it that way. "You tell me."

He had the cockiest grin she'd ever seen. Whenever he used it on her she felt a tremor that she was certain was annoyance. "Dodge City?" she said sweetly. "We don't get many cowboys this far east." She turned and was halfway down the hall when he took her arm.

"Are you always in such a hurry?"

"I don't like to waste time."

He kept his hand on her arm as they continued to walk. "I'll keep that in mind."

My God, the place was fabulous, Sloan thought as they started up a pie-shaped set of steps. Coffered ceilings, carved lintels, thick mahogany paneling. He stopped at an arched window to touch the wavy glass. It had to be original, he thought, like the chestnut floor and the fancy plaster work.

True, there were cracks in the walls—some of them big enough that he could slide his finger in to the first knuckle. Here and there the ceiling had given way to fist-sized holes, and portions of the molding were rotted.

It would be a challenge to bring it back to its former glory. And it would be a joy.

"We haven't used this part of the house in years." Amanda opened a carved oak door and brushed away a spider web. "It hasn't been practical to heat it during the winter."

Sloan stepped inside. The sloping floor creaked ominously as he walked across it. Somewhere along the line heavy furniture had been dragged in or out, scarring the floor with deep, jagged grooves. Two of the panes on the narrow terrace doors had been broken and replaced with plywood. Mice had had a field day with the baseboard. Above his head was a faded mural of chubby cherubs.

"This was the best guest room," Amanda explained. "Fergus kept it for people he wanted to impress. Supposedly some of the Rockefellers stayed here. It has its own bath and dressing room." She pushed open a broken door.

Ignoring her, Sloan walked to the black marble fireplace. The wall above it was papered in silk and stained from old smoke. The chip off the corner of the mantel broke his heart.

"You ought to be shot."

"I beg your pardon?"

"You ought to be shot for letting the place go like this." The look he aimed at her wasn't lazy and amused, but hot and quick as a bullet. "A mantelpiece like this is irreplaceable."

Flustered, she stared guiltily at the chipped Italian marble. "Well, I certainly didn't break it."

"And look at these walls. Plasterwork of this caliber is an art, the same way a Rembrandt is art. You'd take care of a Rembrandt, wouldn't you?"

"Of course, but—"

"At least you had the sense not to paint the molding." Moving past her, he peered into the adjoining bath. And began to swear. "These are handmade tiles, for God's sake. Look at these chips. They haven't been grouted since World War I."

"I don't see what that's—"

"No, you don't see." He turned back to her. "You haven't got a clue to what you've got here. This place

is a monument to early-twentieth-century craftsman-
ship, and you're letting it fall apart around your ears.
Those are authentic gaslight fixtures.''

"I know very well what they are," Amanda snapped
back. "This may be a monument to you, but to me it's
home. We've done everything we could to keep the roof
on. If the plaster's cracked it's because we've had to
concentrate on keeping the furnace running. And if we
didn't worry about regrouting tiles in a room no one
uses, it's because we had to repair the plumbing in another one. You've been hired to renovate, not to phi-
losophize.''

"You get both for the same price." When he reached
out toward her, she rammed back into the wall.

"What are you doing?"

"Take it easy, honey. You've got cobwebs in your
hair.''

"I can do it," she said, then stiffened when he
combed his fingers through her hair. "And don't call
me 'honey.' ''

"You sure fire up quick. I had a mustang filly once
that did the same thing."

She knocked his hand aside. "I'm not a horse."

"No, ma'am." In an abrupt change of mood, he
smiled again. "You sure aren't. Why don't you show
me what else you've got?"

Wary, she eased to the side until she felt safe again.
"I don't see the point. You haven't got a notebook."

"Some things stick in your mind." His gaze lowered to her mouth, lingered, then returned to her eyes.
"I like to get the lay of the land first before I start
worrying about...details."

"Why don't I draw you a map?"

He grinned then. "You always so prickly?"

"No." She inclined her head. It was true, she wasn't. She could hardly have made a success in her career as assistant manager in one of the resort's better hotels if she was. "Obviously you don't bring out the best in me."

"I'll settle for what I've got." He curled a hand around her arm. "Let's keep going."

She took him through the wing, doing her best to keep her distance. But he had a tendency to close in, blocking her in a doorway, maneuvering her into a corner, shifting unexpectedly to put them face-to-face. He had a slow and economical way of moving, wasting no gestures that would tip her off as to which way he was going to turn.

They were in the west tower the third time Amanda bumped into him. Every nerve was on edge when she stepped back. "I wish you wouldn't do that."

"Do what?"

"Be there." Annoyed, she shoved aside a cardboard box. "In my way."

"It seems to me you're in too much of a hurry to get someplace else to watch where you are."

"More homespun philosophy," she muttered, and paced to the curved window that overlooked the gardens. He bothered her, she was forced to admit, on some deep, elemental level. Maybe it was his size— those broad shoulders and wide-palmed hands. His sheer height. She was accustomed to being on a more even level with most men.

Maybe it was that drawl of his, slow and lazy and every bit as cocky as his grin. Or the way his eyes lingered on her face, persistent, with a half-amused gleam. Whatever it was, Amanda thought with a little shake, she would have to learn how to handle it.

"This is the last stop," she told him. "Trent's idea is to convert this tower into a dining room, more intimate than the one he wants on the lower level. It should fit five tables for two comfortably, with views of the garden or the bay."

She turned as she spoke, and an early evening sunbeam shot through the window to halo her hair and pool lustrously around her. Her hands gestured with her words, a graceful flow of movement underlined by nerves. She lifted one hand to her hair to push it back. The light streamed through the honey-brown tresses, tipping them with gold. In the single shaft of light, dust motes danced around her like minute flakes of silver.

His mind wiped clean as new glass, Sloan stood and stared.

"Is something wrong?"

"No." He took a step closer. "You sure are easy on the eyes, Amanda."

She took a step back. There wasn't amusement in his eyes now, or the quick flaring anger she had seen briefly earlier. What was there was a great deal more dangerous. "If you, ah, have any questions about the tower, or the rest of the wing—"

"That was a compliment. Maybe not as smooth as you're used to, but a compliment just the same."

"Thank you." Her eyes darted around the room for a means of dignified escape as she retreated another step. "I think we could—" She ended on a gasp as his arm snaked around her waist to draw her tight against him. "What the hell do you think you're doing?"

"Keeping you from taking the same jump as your great-grandma." He nodded toward the window at her back. "If you'd kept dancing backward, you might have gone right through the glass. Those panes don't look very strong."

"I wasn't dancing anywhere." But her heart was pounding as if she had just finished a fast rumba. "Let go."

"You're a real nice armful." He leaned closer to take a sniff of her hair. "Even with all those thorns." Enjoying himself, he kept his arm where it was. "You could've said thanks, Calhoun. I probably just saved your life."

Her pulse might have been jumping, but she refused to let herself be intimidated by some slow-talking cowboy with an attitude. "If you don't let me go, now, someone's going to have to save yours."

He laughed, delighted with her, and was tempted to scoop her up there and then. The next thing he knew, he was landing on his butt five feet away. With a smug smile, Amanda inclined her head.

"That concludes our tour for this evening. Now, if you'll excuse me." When she started by him, his hand snaked out and snagged her ankle. Amanda barely had time to shriek before she landed on the floor beside him. "Why, you—oaf," she decided, and tossed the hair out of her eyes.

"What's good for the goose is good for the gander." He tipped a fingertip under her chin. "More homespun philosophy. You've got quick moves, Calhoun, but you've got to remember to keep your eye on the target."

"If I were a man—"

"This wouldn't be half as much fun." Chuckling, he gave her a quick, hard kiss, then tilted his head back to stare at her while she gaped. "Well, now," he said softly while lightning bolts went off inside his chest. "I think we'd better try that again."

She would have shoved him away. She knew she would have. Despite the heat trembling along her spine. Regardless of the thick syrupy longing that seemed to have replaced the blood churning in her veins. She would have shoved him away, had even lifted a hand to do so—certainly not to bring him closer—when footsteps clattered on the iron steps that led to the tower.

Sloan glanced up to see a tall, curvy woman in the doorway. She wore jeans that were ripped through at the knee with a plain white T-shirt tucked in the waist. Her hair was short and straight, offset by a fringe of sassy bangs. Below them her eyes registered surprise, then amusement.

"Hi." She looked at Amanda, grinning as she noted her sister's flushed face and tousled hair. The one place you didn't expect to see business-first Amanda Calhoun was on the floor with a strange and very attractive man. "What's going on?"

"We were going for the best two out of three," Sloan told her. He rose, then hauled Amanda up by the arm. With what sounded like a snarl, Amanda jerked out of his hold, then busied herself brushing the dust from her slacks.

"This is my sister, C.C."

"And you must be Sloan." C.C. walked in, offering her hand. "Trent's told me about you." Green eyes dancing, she flicked a glance at her sister, then back again. "I guess he didn't exaggerate."

Sloan held the offered hand a moment. C. C. Calhoun was exactly the opposite of the kind of woman he'd expected his old friend to be involved with. And because Trent was his friend, Sloan couldn't have been more delighted. "I can see why Trent's got himself roped and corralled."

"That's one of Sloan's whimsical compliments," Amanda pointed out.

With a laugh, C.C. threw an arm around Amanda's shoulders. "I think I figured that out. I'm glad to meet you, Sloan. Really glad. When I went up to Boston with Trent a couple of weeks ago, everyone I met was so..."

"Stuffy?" He grinned.

"Well." A little embarrassed, she moved her shoulders. "I guess it's hard for some of them to accept that Trent's going to marry a mechanic who knows more about engines than opera."

"Looks to me like Trent's getting one hell of a deal."

"We'll see." She knew with the least encouragement she would get mushy and embarrass herself. "Aunt Coco said you were staying for dinner. I was hoping you'd take one of the guest rooms here while you're on the island."

Sloan couldn't see it, but he'd have bet the pot that Amanda bit her tongue. The idea of ruffling her feathers made it tempting to change his plans. "Thanks, but I'm all taken care of. Besides..." Now he grinned at Amanda. "I'm going to be underfoot enough as it is."

"However you're most comfortable," C.C. told him. "Just so that you know you're welcome here at The Towers."

"I'll go down and see if Aunt Coco needs any help." Amanda sent Sloan a cool nod. "C.C. will show you down when you're ready."

He winked at her. "Thanks for the tour, honey."

He could almost hear her grinding her teeth as she walked away.

"That's some sister you've got there."

"Yes, she is." C.C.'s smile was warm, and warning. "Trent tells me you're quite the ladies' man."

"He's still mad because I stole a woman out from under his nose when we were both still young and foolish." Sloan took C.C.'s hand as they walked through the doorway. "You sure you're stuck on him?"

She had to laugh. "Now I see why he told me to lock up my sisters."

"If they're anything like that one, I expect they can take care of themselves."

"Oh, they can. The Calhoun women are as tough as they come." She paused at the top of the iron circular stairs. "I'd better warn you. Aunt Coco claims she saw you in the tea leaves this morning."

"In the...aah."

She gave a half apologetic, half amused shrug. "It's kind of a hobby of hers. Anyway, she might start to try to manipulate, especially if she decides the fates have linked you with one of my sisters. She means well, but..."

"O'Rileys are pretty good at handling themselves, too."

It only took one long look at him to have her believing it. C.C. tapped his shoulder. "Okay then. You're on your own."

Sloan started down behind her. "C.C., are there any men Amanda's involved with who I'm going to have to hoist out of the way?"

C.C. stopped, studying him through the opposite side of the open stairs. "No," she said after a moment. "Amanda's done all the hoisting herself."

"That's fine." He was smiling to himself as he descended the winding stairs. When they reached the second floor, he heard an echo of high-pitched screams and the frantic yapping of the dog.

"My sister Suzanna's kids," C.C. explained before he could ask. "Alex and Jenny are your typical quiet, retiring children."

"I can hear that."

A sturdy pale-haired missile zoomed up the steps. In reflex, Sloan caught it and found himself staring into a curious little face with a pouty mouth and big blue eyes.

"You're big," Jenny said.

"Nah. You're just short."

At five, she was just beginning to learn the wiles of womanhood and sent him a beaming smile. "Can I have a piggyback ride?"

"Got a quarter?" Giggling, she shook her head. "Okay," he said, "the first one's free then." When she squirmed around to his back, he started down again. At the base of the steps, Amanda had a dark-haired little boy in a headlock.

"Suzanna?" C.C. asked.

"In the kitchen. I was drafted to watch these two." She narrowed her eyes at Jenny. "The little pig-nosed one got away from me."

"Oink, oink." From the tower of Sloan's back, Jenny giggled and snorted.

"Who's he?" Alex wanted to know.

"Sloan O'Riley." Sloan offered a hand, man to man, which Alex eyed dubiously before accepting it.

"You talk funny. Are you from Texas?"

"Oklahoma."

After a moment's consideration, Alex nodded. "That's almost as good. Did you ever shoot anybody dead?"

"Not lately."

"That's enough, you ghoul." C.C. took charge. "Come on, let's go get cleaned up for dinner." She swung Jenny from Sloan's back.

"Cute kids," Sloan commented when C.C. hauled them up the stairs.

"We like them." Amanda offered him a genuine smile. Seeing him with Jenny riding his back had softened her. "They'll be in school most of the day, so they shouldn't bother you while you're working."

"I don't figure they'd be a bother one way or the other. I've got a nephew of my own back home. He's a pistol."

"Those two can be shotguns, I'm afraid." But the affection came through. "It's nice for them to be around a man now and again."

"Your sister's husband?"

The smile faded. "They're divorced. You might know him. Baxter Dumont?"

A shutter seemed to come down over Sloan's eyes. "I've heard of him."

"Well, that's history. Dinner's nearly ready. Why don't I show you where to wash up?"

"Thanks." Distracted, Sloan followed her. He was thinking that there were some points of history that had an unfortunate habit of overlapping.

Three

___

Anticipating the shock, Amanda dove into the cold water of the pool. She surfaced with a delicious shiver then began the first of her usual fifty laps.

There was nothing she liked better than beginning a day with a vigorous workout. It ate away the old tension to make room for the new that would develop before the workday was done.

Not that she didn't enjoy her job as assistant manager of the BayWatch Hotel. Particularly since it gave her the privilege of using the hotel pool before the guests began to crowd in. It was the end of May and the season had begun to swing. Of course it was nothing compared to what it would be by midsummer, but most of the rooms in the hotel were occupied, which meant she had her hands full. This hour, which she gave herself whenever weather permitted, was prized.

As she approached one end of the pool, she curled, tucked and pushed off.

In another year, she thought as she sent beads of water flying, she would be manager of The Towers Retreat. A St. James hotel. The goal that she had worked and struggled for since she'd taken her first part-time job as a desk clerk at sixteen was about to be realized.

It nagged at her from time to time that she would have the job only because Trent was marrying her sister. Whenever it did, she became only more determined to prove that she deserved it, that she had earned it.

She would be managing an exclusive hotel for one of the top chains in the country. And not just any hotel, she thought, cutting cleanly through the water, but The Towers. A part of her own heritage, her own history, her own family.

The ten luxurious suites Trent intended to create out of the crumbling west wing would be her responsibility. If he was right, the St. James name and the legend of The Towers would keep those suites filled year-round.

She would do a good job. An exceptional one. Every guest who traveled home from The Towers would remember the excellent service, the soothing ambience, the silky smooth organization.

It was going to happen. There would be no more slaving for a demanding and unappreciative supervisor, no more frustration at doing the work and handing over the credit. At last the credit, and the failure, would be hers alone.

It was only a matter of waiting until the remodeling was done.

And that brought her thoughts ramming headfirst into Sloan O'Riley.

She certainly hoped Trent knew what he was doing. What baffled her most was how such a smooth and polished man such as Trenton St. James III had ever become friends with a throwback like O'Riley. The man had actually knocked her down. Of course, she'd knocked him down first, but that was entirely beside the point.

Amanda kicked off again. Her leanly muscled arms sliced through the water, her long legs scissored. She didn't regret, not for a minute, that she'd had the wit and the strength to get the best of him first. He'd been pushy and overfamiliar and too full of himself from the moment she'd met him. And he'd kissed her.

She turned her head up for air then slid her face into the water again.

She hadn't given him the least bit of encouragement. In fact, just the opposite. But he'd sat there, grinning like a fool, and had kissed her. The memory of it had her gasping for air again.

Not that she'd liked it, Amanda assured herself. If C.C. hadn't walked in, she would have given the arrogant Mr. O'Riley a piece of her mind. Except that she hadn't had one left.

Because she'd been angry, that's all. She wasn't a bit attracted to the rough, outdoorsy type with callused hands and dusty boots. She wasn't fool enough to fall for a pair of dark green eyes that crinkled at the corners when they smiled. Her image of the ideal man included a certain sophistication, smooth manners, culture, a quiet aura of success. If and when she became interested in a relationship, those would be her requirements. Slow-talking cowboys need not apply.

Maybe there had been something sweet about him when he'd talked to the children, but it wasn't enough to overcome the rest of the deficits in his personality.

She remembered the way he'd flirted and charmed Aunt Coco at dinner. He'd kept C.C. amused with stories of Trent's college days and had been tolerant and easy with Alex's and Jenny's questions about horses and Indians and six-shooters.

But he'd watched Suzanna a little too closely, a little too carefully for Amanda's liking. A woman chaser, Amanda decided. If Lilah had been at dinner, he probably would have flirted with her, as well. But Lilah could take care of herself where men were concerned.

Suzanna was different. She was beautiful, sensitive and vulnerable. Her ex-husband had hurt her deeply, and no one, not even the cocky Sloan O'Riley was going to get the chance to hurt Suzanna again. Amanda would make sure of it.

When she reached the edge of the pool this time, she gripped the coping and dipped her head back into the water to slick her hair out of her eyes. Surfacing, she found herself staring up into a watery image that was entirely too familiar.

"Morning." Sloan grinned down at her. The sun was at his back, bringing out the reddish tones in his untidy hair. "You got a nice form there, Calhoun."

She blinked her eyes clear. "What the hell are you doing here?"

"Here?" He glanced over his shoulder at the whitewashed hotel. "You could say I'm hanging my hat here." Watching her, he jerked a thumb up and back. "Room 320."

"You're a guest at the BayWatch?" Amanda propped her elbows on the coping. "It figures."

Agreeable, Sloan crouched down. She had the clear creamy Calhoun skin, he noted, particularly striking, and vulnerable, now washed clean of any cosmetics. "Nice way to start the day."

Her full damp mouth turned down in a frown. "It was."

"Since we're asking, what are you doing here?"

"I work here."

Things were becoming more and more interesting, he thought. "No fooling?"

"No fooling," she said dryly. "I'm assistant manager."

"Well, now." He dipped an experimental finger into the water. "Checking out the water temperature for the guests? That's dedication."

"The pool doesn't open until ten."

"Don't worry." He hooked his thumbs in the front pockets of his jeans. "I wasn't planning on taking a dip just yet." What he had been planning was to take a walk, a long solitary one. But that was before he'd spotted her doing laps. "So, I guess if I have any questions about the place, you're the one I talk to."

"That's right." Amanda moved over to the steps to climb out. The one-piece sapphire-colored suit clung like a second skin as water slid from her. "Is your room satisfactory?"

"Hmm?" She had legs designed to make a man sweat, he thought, slim and shapely and a yard long.

"Your room," she repeated as she reached for her towel. "It suits you?"

"It suits me fine. Just fine." He skimmed his gaze up those damp calves and thighs, over the slim hips on a lazy journey to her face. "The view's worth the price of admission."

Amanda hooked the towel around her neck. "The view of the bay's free—like the continental breakfast now being served in The Galley. You'll want to take advantage of it."

"I've found that a couple of croissants and a cup of coffee don't do much to stanch the appetite." Because he wasn't ready for her to walk away, he reached out to take both ends of the towel in a light grip. "Why don't you join me for a real breakfast?"

"Sorry." Her heart was beginning to thud uncomfortably. "Employees are discouraged from socializing with the guests."

"I reckon we could make an exception in this case, seeing as we're... old friends."

"We're not even new friends."

There was that smile again, slow, insistent and all too knowing. And then he said, "That's something we can fix over breakfast."

"Sorry. Not interested." She started to turn away, but he tightened his grip on the towel and held her in place.

"Where I come from people are a mite more friendly."

Since he wasn't giving her a choice, she held her ground. "Where I come from people are a great deal more polite. If you have any problems with the service during your stay at the BayWatch, I'll be more than happy to accommodate you. If you have any questions about The Towers, I'll make myself available to answer them. Other than that, we have nothing to discuss."

He watched her patiently, admiring the way she could coat her husky voice with frost even while her eyes glinted. This was a woman with plenty of control. And, though he was certain she'd snarl at the term, plenty of spunk.

"What time do you go on the clock here?"

She let out a hiss of breath. Obviously the man's head was as thick as his accent. "Nine o'clock, so if you'll excuse me, I'd like to go get dressed."

Sloan squinted up at the sun. "Looks to me like you've got about an hour before you punch in. The way you move, it won't take you half that to get yourself together."

Amanda shut her eyes briefly on a prayer for patience. "Sloan, are you trying to irritate me?"

"Don't figure I have to. It seems to come natural." Casually he wound the ends of the towel around his fists and had her jerking closer. He grinned as her chin shot up. "See?"

She resented bitterly the way her pulse was dancing, and the tight, clutching sensation deep in her stomach. "What's the matter with you, O'Riley?" she demanded. "I've made it absolutely plain that I'm not interested."

"I'll tell you how it is, Calhoun." He flipped his wrists again, shortening the towel farther. The humor she was used to seeing in his eyes changed into something else in the space of a heartbeat. And that something else was dark and dangerous. And exciting. "You're one long, cool drink of water," he murmured. "Every time I'm around you I get this powerful thirst." With a last jerk, he had her tumbling against him, her hands trapped tight between their bodies. "That little sip I had yesterday wasn't nearly enough." Bending down, he nipped at her bottom lip.

He felt her tremor, but as he kept his eyes on hers, he could see it wasn't from fear. A trace of panic maybe, but not fear. Still he waited to see if she would give him a flat-out no. That was something he would have to respect, however much the need churned through him.

But she said nothing, only stared at him with those wide wary eyes. Softly he brushed his lips over hers and watched the thick lashes flutter down. "I want more," he murmured. And took.

Her hands curled into fists between them, but she didn't use them to push him away. The struggle was all inside her, a wild and violent combat that jolted her system even as he bombarded her senses. Caught in the crossfire, her mind simply shut down.

His mouth wasn't lazy now. Nor were his hands slow. Hard and hot, his lips took from hers while his fingers pressed against her damp back. The scrape of his teeth had her gasping, then moaning when his tongue slid seductively over hers.

Her fingers uncurled to clutch at his shirt, then to claw their way up to his shoulder, into his hair. The desperation was new, terrifying, wonderful. It drove her to strain against him while her mouth burned with an urgency that matched his.

The change rocked him. He was used to having his senses clouded by a woman, to having his body throb and his blood burn. But not like this. In the instant she went from dazed surrender to fevered urgency, he knew a need so sharp, so jagged that it seemed to slice through his soul.

Then all he knew was her. All he could feel was the cool slick silk of her skin. All he could taste was the honeyed heat of her mouth. All he could want was more.

She was certain her heart would pound its way out of her breast. It seemed the heat from his body turned the water on her skin to steam, and the vapors floated through her brain. Nor did they clear when he eased her gently away.

"Amanda." He drew in a deep gulp of air but wasn't sure he'd ever get his breath back again. One look at her as she stood heavy eyed, her swollen lips parted, had the edgy desire cutting through him again. "Come up to my room."

"Your room?" She touched unsteady fingers to her lips, then her temple. "Your room?"

Lord, that throaty voice and those dazed eyes were going to have him on his knees. One thing he'd yet to do was beg for a woman. With her, he was afraid begging was inevitable.

"Come with me." Possessively he ran his hands over her shoulders. Somewhere along the line the towel had slid to the concrete. "We need to finish this in private."

"Finish this?"

On a groan, he brought his lips back to hers again in a last, long, greedy kiss. "Woman, I think you're going to be late for work."

He had her arm and had pulled her toward the gate before she shook her head clear. His room? she thought fussily. Finish this? Oh, Lord, what had she done? What was she about to do? "No." She jerked away and took a deep, cleansing breath that did nothing to stop the tremors. "I'm not going anywhere."

He tried to steady himself and failed. "It's a little late to play games." His hand snaked out to cup the back of her neck. "I want you. And there's no way in hell you're going to convince me you don't want me right back. Not after that."

"I don't play games," she said evenly, and wondered if he could hear her over the riot of her heartbeat. She was cold, so terribly cold. "I don't intend to start now." She was the sensible one, she reminded herself. She wasn't the kind of woman who raced into a hotel room to make love with a man she barely knew. "I want you to leave me alone."

"Not a chance." He struggled to keep his fingers light as temper and need warred inside him. "I always finish what I start."

"You can consider this finished. It had no business starting."

"Why?"

She turned away to snatch up her wrap. The thin terry cloth wasn't nearly enough to warm her again. "I know your type, O'Riley."

He reached deep for calm and rocked back on his heels. "Do you?"

Clumsy with temper, she fought to push her arms through the sleeves. "You swagger from town to town and fill a few free hours with an available woman having a quick roll between the sheets." She pulled the tie on the wrap tight. "Well, I'm not available."

"You figure you got me pegged, huh?" He didn't touch her, but the look in his eyes was enough to have her bracing. He didn't bother to explain that it was different with her. He hadn't yet explained it to himself. "You can take this as a warning, Calhoun. This isn't finished between us. I'm going to have you."

"Have me? *Have* me." Propelled by pride and fury, she took one long stride toward him. "Why you conceited self-absorbed sonofabitch—"

"You can save the flattery for later," he interrupted. "There will be a later, Amanda, when it's just you and me. And I promise you, it won't be quick." Because the idea appealed to him, he smiled. "No sir, when I make love with you, I'm going to take my time." He ran a finger down the collar of her wrap. "And I'm going to drive you crazy."

She slapped his hand away. "You already are."

"Thanks." He gave her a friendly nod. "I think I'll go see about that breakfast. You have a good day."

She would, she thought as he walked off whistling. She'd have a fine day if he was out of it.

It was bad enough that she had to work late, Amanda thought, without having to listen to one of Mr. Stenerson's droning lectures on efficiency. As manager of the BayWatch, Stenerson ruled his staff with fussy hands and whines. His preferred method of supervision was to delegate. In that way he could dole out blame when things went wrong, and gather in credit when things went right.

Amanda stood in his airy pastel office, staring at the top of his balding head as he ran through his weekly list of complaints.

"Housekeeping has been running behind by twenty minutes. In my spot check of the third floor, I discovered this cellophane wrapper under the bed of 302." He waved the tiny clear paper like a flag. "I expect you to have a better handle on things, Miss Calhoun."

"Yes, sir." *You officious little wienie.* "I'll speak to the housekeeping staff personally."

"See that you do." He lifted his ever-present clipboard. "Room service speed is off by eight percent. At this rate of deterioration, it will lower to twelve percent by the height of the season."

Unlike Stenerson, Amanda had done time in the kitchen during the breakfast and dinner rush. "Perhaps if we hired another waiter or two," she began.

"The solution is not in adding more staff, but in culling more efficiency from those we have." He tapped a finger on the clipboard. "I expect to see room service up to maximum by the end of next week."

"Yes, sir." *You supercilious windbag.*

"I'll expect you to roll up your sleeves and pitch in whenever necessary, Miss Calhoun." He folded his soft white hands and leaned back. Before he'd opened his mouth again, Amanda knew what was coming. She could have recited the speech by rote.

"Twenty-five years ago, I was delivering trays to guests in this very hotel. It was through sheer determination and a positive outlook that I worked my way up to the position I hold today. If you expect to succeed, perhaps even take over in this office after my retirement, you must eat, sleep and drink the BayWatch. The efficiency of the staff directly reflects your efficiency, Miss Calhoun."

"Yes, sir." She wanted to tell him that in another year she would have her own staff, her own office and he could kiss his whipping boy goodbye. But she didn't tell him. Until that time, she needed the job and the weekly paycheck. "I'll have a meeting with the kitchen staff right away."

"Good, good. Now, I'll want you on call this evening, as I'll be incommunicado."

As always, she thought but murmured her agreement.

"Oh, and check the August reservations. I want a report on the ratio of Escape Weekends to Seven-Day Indulgences. Oh, and speak with the pool boy about missing towels. We're five short already this month."

"Yes, sir." Anything else? she wondered. Shine your shoes, wash your car?

"That'll be all."

Amanda opened the door and struggled to keep her unflappable professional mask in place. All she really wanted to do was knock her head against the wall for a few indulgent minutes. Before she could retreat to some private, quiet place to do so, she was called to the front desk.

Sloan took a seat in the lobby just to watch her. He was surprised to see that she was still working. He'd put in a full day at The Towers, and the scarred briefcase beside the chair was bulging with notes, measurements and sketches. He was ready for a tall beer and a rare steak.

But here she was, soothing guests, instructing desk clerks, signing papers. And looking just as cool and fresh as spring water. He watched her pull off an earring, jiggling it in her palm as she took a phone call.

It was one of life's small pleasures to watch her, he decided. All that drive and energy, the effortless control. Almost effortless, he thought with a grin. There was a line between her brows—frustration, he thought. Annoyance. Or just plain stubbornness. He had a powerful urge to go up to her and smooth it away. Instead, he gestured to a bellman.

"Yes, sir."

"Is there a florist around here?"

"Yes, sir, just down the street."

Still watching Amanda, Sloan dug out his wallet and pulled out a twenty. "Would you run down there and get me a red rose? A long-stemmed one that's still closed. And keep the change."

"Yes, *sir*. Thank you, sir."

While he waited, Sloan ordered a beer from the lobby bar and lighted a cigar. Stretching out his booted feet, he settled back to enjoy.

Amanda clipped on her earring then pressed a hand to her stomach. At least when she went down to give the kitchen staff a pep talk she could grab something to eat. A glance at her watch told her that she wouldn't have time to take her evening shift going through the paperwork, looking for a clue to the necklace. If there was any bright side to the enforced overtime, it was that Sloan wouldn't be at The Towers when she returned.

"Excuse me."

Amanda glanced up to see a trim, attractive man in a bone-colored suit. His dark hair was brushed back from a high forehead. Pale blue eyes smiled pleasantly as they looked into hers. The faint British accent added charm to his voice.

"Yes, sir. May I help you?"

"I'd like to speak with the manager."

Amanda felt her heart sink a little. "I'm sorry, Mr. Stenerson is unavailable. If there's a problem, I'll be glad to handle it for you."

"No problem, Miss—" his eyes flicked down to her name tag "—Calhoun. I'll be checking in for a few weeks. I believe I have the Island Suite."

"Of course. Mr. Livingston. We're expecting you." Quick and competent, she tapped the information into the computer herself. "Have you stayed with us before?"

"No." He smiled again. "Regrettably."

"I'm sure you'll find the suite very comfortable." She passed him a registration form as she spoke. "If there's anything we can do to make your stay more pleasant, don't hesitate to ask."

"I'm already certain it will be pleasant." He gave her another lingering look as he filled out the form. "Unfortunately, it must also be productive. I wanted to inquire about the possibility of renting a fax machine during my stay."

"We offer fax service for our guests' convenience," she said.

"I'll require my own." The diamond on his pinky winked as he slid the form across the counter. "I'm afraid I wasn't able to clear up all my business, as I had hoped. It simply wouldn't be practical for me to run down here every time I need to send or receive a document. Naturally, I'll be willing to pay whatever necessary for the convenience. If renting isn't feasible, perhaps I can purchase one."

"I'll see what I can arrange."

"I'd appreciate that." He offered her his credit card for an imprint. "Also, I'll be using the parlor in the suite as an office. I'd prefer if housekeeping left my papers and disarray undisturbed."

"Of course."

"Might I ask if you're familiar with the island?"

Smiling, she handed him his card and his keys. "I'm a native."

"Wonderful." His eyes on hers, he held her hand lightly. "Then I'll know to come to you if I have any questions. You've been very helpful, Miss Calhoun."

He glanced at her name tag again. "Amanda. Thank you."

"You're quite welcome." Her pulse gave a quick jitter as she slid her hand from his to signal a bellman. "Enjoy your stay, Mr. Livingston."

"I already am."

As he walked away, the young desk clerk beside Amanda gave a low feminine sigh. "Who was that?"

"William Livingston." Amanda caught herself staring after him and pulled herself back to file the imprint.

"Gorgeous. If he had looked at me the way he looked at you, I'd have melted on the spot."

"Melting's not part of the job description, Karen."

"No." Dreamy eyed, Karen put her hand on a ringing phone. "But it sure is part of being a woman. Front desk, Karen speaking. May I help you?"

William Livingston, Amanda thought, tapping his registration form against her palm. New York, New York. If he could afford a couple of weeks in the Island Suite, that meant he had money as well as charm, good looks and impeccable taste in clothes. If she'd been looking for a man, he would have fit the bill nicely.

Opening up the phone book, Amanda reminded herself she was looking for a fax machine, not a man.

"Hey, Calhoun."

With her finger on Office Supplies in the business section, she glanced up. Sloan, his chambray shirt rolled up to the elbows, his hair curling untidily over its collar, leaned on the counter.

"I'm busy," she said dismissively.

"Working late?"

"Good guess."

"You sure look pretty in that little suit." He reached over the counter to rub a thumb and finger down the crisp red lapel of her jacket. "Kinda prim and proper."

Unlike the little bounce her pulse had given when William Livingstone had taken her hand, it went haywire at Sloan's touch. Annoyed, she brushed it away. "Do you have a problem with your room?"

"Nope. It's pretty as a picture."

"With the service?"

"Slick as a wet rock."

"Then if you'll excuse me, I've got work to do."

"Oh, I figured that. I've been watching you tow the mark here for the last half hour."

The line appeared between her brows. "You've been watching me?"

His gaze lingered on her mouth as he remembered just how it tasted. "It made the beer go down easy."

"It must be nice to have so much free time. Now—"

"It's not how much, it's what you do with it. Since you were . . . tied up for breakfast, why don't we have dinner?"

Well aware that her co-workers had their ears pricked, Amanda leaned closer and kept her voice low. "Can't you get it through your head that I'm not interested?"

"No." He grinned, then sent a wink toward Karen, who was hovering as close as discretion allowed. "You said you didn't like to waste time. So I figured we could have a little supper and pick up where we left off this morning."

In his arms, she thought, lost for a moment. With her mind fuddled and her blood racing. She was staring at his mouth when it curved and snapped her back to reality. "I'm busy, and I have no desire—"

"You've got plenty of that, Amanda."

She set her teeth, wishing with all her heart she could call him a liar and mean it. "I don't want to have dinner with you. Clear?"

"As glass." He flicked a finger down her nose. "I'll be upstairs if you get hungry. Three-twenty, remember?" He lifted the rose from behind the counter and put it into her hand. "Don't work too hard."

"Two winners in one night," Karen murmured, and watched Sloan walk away. "Lord, he sure knows how to wear jeans, doesn't he?"

Indeed he did, Amanda thought, then cursed herself. "He's crude, annoying and intolerable." But she brushed the rosebud against her cheek.

"Okay, I'll take bachelor number two. You can concentrate on Mister Beautiful from New York."

Damn it, why was she so breathless? "I'm going to concentrate on my job," Amanda corrected. "And so are you. Stenerson's on the warpath, and the last thing I need is some cowboy stud interrupting my routine."

"I wish he'd offer to interrupt mine," Karen murmured, then bent over her terminal.

She wasn't going to think about him, Amanda promised herself. She set the rose aside, then picked it up again. It wasn't the flower's fault, after all. It deserved to be put in water and appreciated for what it was. Softening a bit, she sniffed at it and smiled. And it had been sweet of him to give it to her. No matter how annoying he might be, she should have thanked him.

Absently she lifted the phone as it rang. "Front desk, Amanda speaking. May I help you?"

"I just wanted to hear you say that." Sloan chuckled into the phone. "Good night, Calhoun."

Biting back an oath, Amanda banged down the receiver. For the life of her she couldn't understand why she was laughing when she took the rose back into her office to find a vase.

I ran to him. It was as if another woman burst out into the twilight to race over the lawn, down the slope, over the rocks. In that moment there was no right or wrong, no duty but to my own heart. Indeed, it was my heart that guided my legs, my eyes, my voice.

He had turned back to the sea. The first time I had seen him he had been facing the sea, fighting his own personal war with paint and canvas. Now he only stared out at the water.

When I called to him, he spun around. In his face I could see the mirror of my own joy. There was laughter, mine and his, as he rushed toward me.

His arms went around me, so tightly. My dreams had known what it would be like to finally be held by them. His mouth fitted truly to mine, so sweet, so urgent.

Time does not stop. As I sit here and write this, I know that. But then, oh then, it did. There was only the wind and the sound of the sea and the sheer and simple glory of being in his arms. It was as if I had waited my entire life, sleeping, eating, breathing, all for the purpose of that single precious window of time. If I have another hundred years left to me, I will never forget an instant of it.

He drew away, his hands sliding down my arms to grip mine, then to bring them to his lips. His eyes were so dark, like gray smoke.

"I'd packed," he said. *"I'd made arrangements to sail to England. Staying here without you was hell. Thinking you would come back, and that I'd never be able to touch you nearly drove me mad. Every day, every night, Bianca, I've ached for you."*

My hands moved over his face, tracing it as I'd often longed to. *"I thought I'd never see you again. I tried to pray that I wouldn't."* As shame crept through my joy, I tried to turn away. *"Oh, what you must think of me. I'm another man's wife, the mother of his children."*

"Not here." His voice was rough, even as his hands were gentle. *"Here you belong to me. Here, where I first saw you a year ago. Don't think of him."*

He kissed me again, and I could not think, could not care.

"I've waited for you, Bianca, through the chill of winter, the warmth of spring. When I tried to paint, it was your image that haunted me. I could see you standing here, with the wind in your hair, the sunlight turning it copper, then gold, then flame. I tried to forget you." His hands were on my shoulders, holding me back while his eyes seemed to devour my face. *"I tried to tell myself it was wrong, that for your sake if not my own, I should leave here. I would think of you, with him, dancing at a ball, attending the theater, taking him into your bed."* His fingers tightened on my shoulders. *"She is his wife, I would tell myself. You have no right to want her, to wish that she would come to you. That she could belong to you."*

I lifted my fingers to his lips. His pain was my pain. I think it will always be so. *"I have come to you,"* I told him. *"I do belong to you."*

He turned away from me, the struggle between con-science and love as strong in him as it was in me. "I have nothing to offer you."

"Your love. There is nothing else I want."

"It's already yours, has been yours from the first moment I looked at you." He came back to me to touch my cheek. I could see the regret, and the long-ing, in those beautiful eyes. "Bianca, there is no fu-ture for us. I cannot and will not ask you to give up what you have."

"Christian—"

"No. Whatever wrongs I do, I will not do that. I know you would give me what I ask, what I have no right to ask, then come to hate me for it."

"No." Tears came to my eyes then, bitter in the cooling wind. "I could never hate you."

"Then I would hate myself." He crushed my fin-gers against his lips again. "But I'll ask you for the summer, for a few hours when you can come here and we can pretend winter will never be." He smiled and kissed me softly. "Come here and meet me, Bianca, in the sunlight. Let me paint you. I'll be content with that."

And so tomorrow, and every day during this sweet, endless summer I will go to him. On the cliffs above the sea we will take what happiness we can.

Four

***

"Well, hello."

At the husky greeting, Sloan looked up from his notes on the billiard room to see a willowy gypsy in a flowing flowered robe. Long cables of red hair streamed down her shoulders and back. Dreamy green eyes assessed him before she glided into the room like a woman who had all the time in the world and was willing to spend it generously.

"Hi." Sloan caught the elusive scent—like crushed wildflowers—before she offered a hand.

"I'm Lilah." Her voice was as lazily flirtatious as her eyes. "We've missed each other the past couple of days."

If there was a man who didn't get a jolt from this one, Sloan thought, he was dead and buried. "I'm real sorry about that."

She laughed then gave his hand a companionable squeeze. First impressions ranked high with Lilah, and she'd already decided to like him. "Me, too. Especially now. What have you been up to?"

"Getting a feel for the place, and the people in it. How about you?"

"I've been busy trying to figure out if I was in love."

"And?"

"Nope." She moved her shoulders gently, but he caught the wistful look in her eyes before she turned to move around the room. "So, what's the plan here, Sloan O'Riley?"

"Elegant dining in a turn-of-the-century atmosphere." He kicked back in the Windsor armchair he'd been using and gestured toward the papers spread over the library table. "We take out part of that wall there, open up into the adjoining study, add a couple of glass pocket doors, and we've got a lounge."

"Just like that?"

"Just like that—after we deal with the structural hassles. I'll have some preliminary sketches for your family and Trent to look over in a couple of days."

"It seems strange," she murmured, running a finger along the old, dusty chair rail. "Thinking about this place being fresh and new again, having people in it." But if she closed her eyes, she could see it perfectly, the way it had once been. "They used to give huge parties, very elaborate, very chic. I can imagine my great-grandfather standing here beside a billiard table sipping Scotch, and wheeling and dealing." She turned back to Sloan. "Do you think about those things when you make your sketches and calculate stress and space?"

"As a matter of fact, I do. There's a burn mark on the floor right over there." He tipped his pencil toward the spot. "I imagine some fat guy in a dinner suit dropped his cigar while he was discussing the war in Europe. A couple of others were standing by the window, stripped down to their shirtsleeves and swirling brandy while they talked about the stock market."

Laughing, Lilah crossed back to him. "And the ladies were down in the parlor."

"Listening to piano music and gossiping about the latest fashions from Paris."

Lilah tilted her head. "Or discussing the possibility of being given the vote."

"There you go."

"I think you're just what The Towers needs," she decided. "Can I take a look at your drawings, or are you temperamental?"

"I make it a policy never to turn down a beautiful woman."

"Astute and clever." She went to lean over his shoulder and push through his papers. "Why, it's the Emperor's Room."

"The what?"

"The Emperor's Room, that's what I call the best guest room. Must be the harps and cherubs on the ceiling." Sliding her hair behind her shoulder, she leaned closer. "This is great."

The dressing room would be a cozy parlor, she noted, complete with a wet bar and an entertainment center that would be hidden behind the original paneling. The bath would remain almost as it was, with the addition of a private whirlpool tucked away in what had been an old storage closet.

"Both ends of one century," Lilah murmured. "You've hardly changed any of the original layout."

"Trent indicated he wanted to keep the luxury and convenience without altering the mood. We'll save most of the original materials, duplicate what's beyond hope."

"You're going to do it." And because she could see that as well, quite clearly, her eyes filled as she laid a hand on his shoulder. "My father wanted to. My mother and he used to talk about it all the time. I wish they could have seen this."

Touched, Sloan laid his hand over hers. Their fingers had linked when Amanda came to the door. Her first reaction was shock at seeing her sister with her cheek all but brushing Sloan's. Then came the spear of jealousy. There was no denying there was something private, even intimate passing between them. On the heels of that sharp green shaft, pride stepped in.

Hadn't she told herself he was a woman chaser?

"Excuse me." Her voice was a thin sheet of ice as she stepped into the room. "I've been looking for you, Lilah."

"You found me." She blinked back the tears but didn't bother to straighten. "I thought I'd come by and meet Sloan."

"I see you have." Determined to be casual if it killed her, Amanda jammed her hands into the pockets of her sweats. "It's your turn for a shift in the storeroom."

"That's what I get for having the day off." She wrinkled her nose, then sent Sloan a smile. "The Calhouns have become detectives, searching for clues to the hiding place of the elusive emeralds."

"So I've heard."

"Maybe you'll take a hack at one of the walls, and they'll fall out, looking as fabulous and glittery as the day Bianca hid them." With a sigh, she drew away. "Well, since duty calls, I'd better get dressed for it. Mandy, you ought to take a look at some of Sloan's sketches. They're great."

"I'll bet."

The tone would have been a direct tip-off, even if Lilah hadn't known her sister so well. So, Lilah thought with a lifted brow. That's the way it was. Since she'd never been able to resist teasing her sister, she leaned down to kiss Sloan's cheek. "Welcome to The Towers."

He didn't have a doubt as to what she was up to. The eyes might be dreamy, he thought, but there was a shrewd and devilish brain behind them. "Thanks. I'm feeling more at home every day."

"I'll meet you in the sweatshop in fifteen minutes," she said to Amanda, then grinned to herself as she went out.

"Is that your new uniform?" he asked Amanda as she stood scowling in the center of the room, her hands still fisted in the pockets of baggy gray sweats.

"I don't go in until two today."

"That's nice." He crossed his outstretched legs at the ankles. "I like your sister."

"That was obvious."

He only grinned. "What does she do, anyway?"

"If you mean professionally, she's a naturalist at Acadia National Park."

"Wildflowers and stuff. It suits."

As if the admiration in his voice didn't bother her in the least, she shrugged and walked to the terrace doors. "I thought you'd be taking measurements or something." Glancing over her shoulder, she shot him a narrow look. "Of the rooms, that is."

This time he laughed outright. "You're mighty cute when you're jealous, Calhoun."

Now she turned to look deliberately down her nose. "I don't know what you're talking about."

"Sure you do, but you can relax. I've already set my sights on you."

Did he expect her to be flattered? she wondered. The hell of it was that, in a odd way, she was. "Do I look like a target?"

"I'd say more like the grand prize." In a gesture of peace, he held up a hand as she sucked in her breath to swear at him. "Before you get more fired up, why don't we deal with business?"

"I am not fired up," she lied. "And I don't see what business we could have."

"Trent said you were the one I should…collaborate with, until he got back. Seeing as you're the one who handles most of the family business, and you've got a firsthand knowledge of hotels."

Because it was logical, she calmed enough to consider it. "What do you want to know?"

How long it's going to take me to knock down that wall around you, he thought. "I figured you'd want to take a look at what I've started. I'd like to get to the drawing board soon."

Actually she was dying to see, but kept her agreement grudgingly cool. "All right, but I only have a few minutes."

"I'll take what I can get."

He waited as she crossed the room. She didn't trust him worth spit, Sloan decided. And that was just fine for now.

"I've got two of the suites mapped out," he told her, shuffling papers. "Plus the tower and most of the dining room here."

She leaned closer, squinting a bit to focus without her reading glasses. As Lilah had been, she was impressed with the sketches. Not only were they competent, but they showed a quick understanding of mood, tone and the practicality necessary for smooth service.

"You work fast," she said, surprised.

"When it's called for." He enjoyed watching the way she lifted a hand to tuck back the swing of hair, not with the sinuous movements of her redheaded sister, but with a quick, absent flick. She smelled of soap and some cool sprinkle of scent.

"What's this?"

"What's what?" He was too busy with the way the sunlight showered on her hair to pay attention to anything else.

"This." She tapped a finger on a sketch.

"Hmm. That's an old servants' stairway. We bring this wall out here, to box it in." He took her finger to slide it along the sketch, the rough side of his palm fitting over the smooth skin of her hand. "It makes this suite two levels, the sitting room and bath down here, two bedrooms and a master bath up here. Since the stairs are already open, it gives us a separation of functions without closing off the flow of space."

"It's nice." Vaguely uneasy with the contact, she flexed her hand but only succeeded in tangling her fingers with his. "I suppose you're going to get estimates and bids."

"I've made some calls."

Something seemed to be happening to her legs from the knees down. They'd gone weak on her, as if she'd run a very long, very fast race. "Well, you..." She braced and turned her head to face him. His eyes were very close, very quiet, very calm. "Obviously you know what you're doing."

"Yeah, I do."

Oh, yeah, he did, she thought as she felt herself pulled toward him—not by his hand, but by something soft and warm and needy inside her. She had only to give in to it, to lean a little closer. Her mouth could be on his, and she would know, as she had known the day before, a kind of whippy excitement and dazzling pleasure. He was waiting, watching her, with those dark green eyes going from calm to intense, willing her to make that slight and significant move. As she began to slide toward him, she heard herself sigh.

Then she remembered.

He had been in almost this same position with Lilah just moments before. Faces close, fingers linked. Only a fool let herself be manipulated by a man who was that casual with a woman's feelings. And Amanda Kelly Calhoun was no fool.

She jerked back, tugging her hand from under his. Sloan felt the knots already winding through his stomach yank tighter.

"Did I miss something?" he asked with a casualness that cost him dearly.

"I don't know what you mean."

"The hell you don't. You were a hair's breadth away from kissing me, Mandy. Your eyes were full of it. Now you've got them frosted up again."

She wished it was as easy to put the ice back into her blood. "You're letting your ego get the best of you. But then, that's probably typical. If you want to take time out to flirt and snuggle with a woman, try Lilah again."

He was used to holding on to his temper. When a man had a dangerous one, he learned early to keep it chained down. But it wasn't easy, not with her, not with the way she so consistently racked his system. "Are you telling me that Lilah's available to any man who asks?"

She went from frost to fire so quickly he could only stare in amazed appreciation. "You don't know anything about my sister, O'Riley. Watch what you say or you'll find yourself on your butt again."

"I was asking what you said," he reminded her.

"I can say what I like, you can't. Lilah has a warm, generous heart. If you do anything to hurt her, I'll—"

"Hold on." Chuckling, he threw up both hands, palms out. "I don't mind you taking a chunk out of me, Calhoun, but I'd rather it be for something I did— or was at least planning to do. First, I'm not quite the tomcat you seem to think I am. And second, I'm not interested in—what was it—snuggling with Lilah."

Amanda's chin lifted a fraction higher. "What's the matter with her?"

Exasperated, he let his hands fall again. "Not a damn thing. Tell me, has your great-grandaddy's insanity trickled down or are you just being plain obstinate?"

"Take your pick." Now she was as embarrassed as she was angry and stalked over to the window to stare out. Whether he was a tomcat—as he'd put it—or not, it was no concerns of hers. It was her problem that she had overreacted to his meeting with Lilah. She was getting herself wound up over nothing, Amanda told herself. If she kept snapping at him every time they spent five minutes together, their business relationship would suffer. And business was, after all, her strongest suit. She gave herself another moment to be sure she'd regained some balance, then turned back.

"We seem to have gotten offtrack. Let's put this back on a professional level, and keep it there."

"You do that real well," he observed.

"What?"

"Pull yourself in. It can't be easy if being around me churns you up half as much as I get being around you." Then he grinned and recrossed his ankles. "Go ahead, be professional. I got real admiration for that side of you."

She wasn't sure whether to scream or laugh or just throw her hands up in defeat. Instead she shook her head and tried again. "I like your work."

"Thanks."

"Trent and I have discussed the budget for the project. He and C.C. may still be on their honeymoon when the bids start coming in. If that's the case, you and I will have to go over them. As far as the hotel section goes, you have a free hand. As to the other part of the house, the family part, we're only interested in essential repairs."

"Why? The place deserves a decent face-lift."

"Because the hotel is a business, and the Calhouns and St. Jameses will be partners. We have the property, he has the funds. We've all agreed that we won't take advantage of his generosity, or the fact that he's marrying C.C."

Sloan considered a moment. "Trent seems to have other ideas. And I've never known him to let anyone take advantage."

The smile softened her face. "I know, and we, all of us, appreciate that he's willing to help, but we feel strongly about this. The Towers, our part of it, is a Calhoun problem. Our position is that we'll accept the needed repairs to the plumbing, the wiring and other immediate necessities, then we'll pay him back from our share of the retreat. If business is good, we'll be able to take care of the rest ourselves within the next few years."

There was pride at stake here, he noted. And more, integrity. He nodded. "You work things out with Trent. Meanwhile, I'll concentrate on the west wing."

"Fine. If your schedule allows, you can take a look at the rest. It would be helpful if we had an idea what the budget will be on the family areas."

He started to point out that he was an architect not a contractor, then shrugged. It wouldn't hurt him to take a look. "Sure. I'll work up an estimate."

"I'd appreciate it. Once you do, I'd prefer if you gave it to me. Just me."

"You're the boss."

She lifted a brow. Odd, but she hadn't thought about it quite that way before. Her lips curved as she digested it. "Then we understand each other. One more thing."

He linked his hands behind his head. "We can have as many things as you want."

"Only one," she said, though her lips quivered. "When I was finalizing some of the wedding plans, I realized you were down as best man. I left your list with Aunt Coco."

"My list?"

"Yes, of the timetable, the duties you're responsible for, that sort of thing. There's also a copy of the necessary information—the name and phone number of the photographer, the contact for the musicians, the bartender we hired…oh, and I jotted down the names of three shops where you can rent a tux." Once again she took in the sheer size of him. "You really should get in for a fitting right away."

"I've got it covered." Impressed, he shook his head. "You're damn efficient, Calhoun."

"Yes, I am. Well then, I'll let you get back to work. I'll be in the third-floor storeroom in the other wing until about one. After that you can reach me at the BayWatch if you have any questions."

"Oh, I know where to find you, Calhoun. Good hunting."

He watched her walk away, and thought of her sitting in the storeroom, surrounded by dusty boxes and mounds of yellowing papers. She'd probably already found a way to put things in their tidy place, he thought with a grin. He wondered if she realized what a sweet contrast it was. She would stack and catalogue and file in the most practical way possible, while she searched through pieces of the past for an old dream.

Amanda found no dreams that morning. By the time she arrived at the BayWatch, she had already put in a five-hour day. When she had started the quest for the necklace weeks before, she had promised herself she wouldn't become discouraged, no matter how long it took or how little she found.

Thus far, they had come across the original receipt for the emeralds, and a date book where Bianca had mentioned them. It was enough, Amanda had decided, to prove the necklace had indeed existed, and to keep hope alive that it would be found again.

She often wondered about it, about what it had meant to Bianca Calhoun and why she had secreted it away. If indeed she had. Another old rumor was that Fergus had tossed the necklace into the sea. After all the stories Amanda had heard about Fergus Calhoun's abiding love of a dollar, it was hard to believe that he had willfully thrown away a quarter of a million in jewels.

Besides, she didn't want to believe it, Amanda admitted as she pinned on her name tag. Though she wouldn't have cared for anyone to know it, she had a strong streak of the romantic, and that part of her held tight to the notion that Bianca had hidden away the emeralds, like a gift or promise, waiting for the time they would be needed again.

It embarrassed her a little to know she felt that way. Amanda preferred the outward, and the logical, routine of sorting through papers and organizing them in the practical pursuit of a valuable heirloom.

Bianca herself remained as much a mystery to Amanda as the necklace. Her ingrained pragmatism made it impossible to understand a woman who had risked everything for, and ultimately had died for, love. Feelings that intense and that desperate seemed unlikely to her, unless they were in the pages of a book.

What would it be like to love that strongly? she wondered. To feel as though your life were so completely bound to another's that it was impossible to survive without him. Inconvenient, she decided. Uncomfortable and unwise. She could only be grateful that she hadn't inherited that dangerous kind of passion. Feeling smug about her own unbattered heart, she settled down to work.

"Amanda?"

She was halfway through the August reservations and held up a hand. "Minute," she murmured, and totaled her calculations to that point. "What is it, Karen? Wow." She pushed her glasses back up her nose and studied the luxurious spray of roses in the desk clerk's arms. "What did you do, win a beauty pageant?"

"They're not mine." Karen buried her face in them. "Don't I wish. They just came in, for you."

"Me?"

"You're still Amanda Calhoun," Karen pointed out as she offered the florist's card. "Though if you want to trade places until these three dozen long-stemmed beauties fade, I'm game."

"Three dozen?"

"I counted." Grinning, Karen laid them on the desk. "Three dozen and one," she added, nodded toward the single rose that stood beside them.

Sloan, Amanda thought, and felt her heart give a quick, catchy sigh. How was she supposed to get a handle on a man who did sweet, unexpected things every time she thought she'd made up her mind about him? How could he have known about her secret weakness for red roses? She hadn't even thanked him for the first one.

"Aren't you going to read the card?" Karen demanded. "If I have to go back to the desk without knowing who sent them, I'll be distracted and my work will suffer. The evil Albert Stenerson'll fire me, and it'll be your fault."

"I already know who they're from," she began, unaware of the softness in her eyes. "It was really so sweet of him to—oh." Baffled, she studied the name on the card. Not Sloan, she realized, with a cutting edge of disappointment that surprised her. They weren't from Sloan.

"Well? Do you want me to beg?"

Still puzzled, Amanda handed the card over.

"*With my appreciation. William Livingston.* Whew." Karen tossed back her long, dark hair. "What did you have to do to deserve this kind of gratitude?"

"I got him a fax machine."

"You got him a fax machine," Karen repeated, handing the card back to Amanda. "Last Sunday I cooked a pot roast with all the trimmings and all I got was a bottle of cheap wine."

Amanda continued to frown and tapped the card on the edge of her desk. "I guess I'd better thank him."

"I guess you'd better." Karen picked up one of the roses and sniffed. "Unless you'd rather delegate. I'd be glad to go up and express your appreciation to Mr. Eyes-To-Die-For Livingston."

"Thanks, but I'll handle it." She picked up the phone, then sent Karen an arched look. "Scram."

"Spoilsport." Laughing, she went out, discreetly shutting the door at her back as Amanda dialed the extension for the Island Suite.

"Livingston."

"Mr. Livingston, this is Amanda Calhoun."

"Ah, the efficient Miss Calhoun." There was a laugh in his voice, a pleasant and flattering one. "What can I do for you?"

"I wanted to thank you for the flowers. They're beautiful. It was very thoughtful of you."

"Just a small way of showing you that I appreciate your help, and the quick work."

"That's my job. Please let me know if I can be of any further assistance during your stay."

"As a matter of fact, there is something you could help me with."

"Of course." Automatically she picked up a pen and prepared to write.

"I'd like you to have dinner with me."

"Excuse me?"

"I'd like to take you to dinner. Eating alone is unappetizing."

"I'm sorry, Mr. Livingston, it's against hotel policy for the staff to socialize with the guests. It's kind of you to ask."

"Kindness has nothing to do with it. Can I ask if you'd consider it if hotel policy could be . . . bent?"

There was no chance of that, Amanda thought. Not with Stenerson. "I'd be happy to consider it," she said tactfully. "Unfortunately, as long as you're a guest at the BayWatch—"

"Yes, yes. I'll get back to you shortly."

Amanda blinked at the dead receiver, shrugged, then replaced it to get back to work. Ten minutes later, Stenerson was opening her door.

"Miss Calhoun, Mr. Livingston would like to have dinner with you." His mouth primed up even more than usual. "You're free to go. Naturally, I'll expect you to conduct yourself in a manner that will reflect properly on the hotel."

"But—"

"Don't make a habit of it."

"I—" But he was already shutting the door. Amanda was still staring at it when her phone rang. "Miss Calhoun."

"Shall we say eight o'clock?"

On a long breath, she sat back in her chair. She was on the point of refusing when she caught herself

stroking the single rosebud Sloan had given her.
Amanda snatched back her hand and balled it in her
lap.

"I'm sorry, I'm on until ten tonight."

"Tomorrow then. Where shall I pick you up?"

"Tomorrow's fine," she said on impulse. "Let me
give you directions."

Five

***

Sloan knew the minute Trent returned to The Towers. Even in the library at the end of a long corridor he could hear the high happy yaps of the dog, the shouts of children and the mix of laughter. Setting aside his notebook, he strolled out to see his old friend.

Trent had gotten no further than the foyer. Jenny was hanging on his legs as Fred circled and danced. Alex was jumping up and down in a bid for attention while Coco, Suzanna and Lilah all fired questions at once. C.C. only stood beaming, held snug against Trent's side. At a shout from above, Sloan looked up to see Amanda bolting down the stairs. Her laughter glowed in her face as he'd never seen it before. Squeezing through her sisters, she took her turn at a hug.

"If you hadn't come back today, I was sending out a team of mercenaries," she told Trent. "Four days before the wedding and you're down in Boston."

"I knew you could handle the details."

"She has miles of lists," Coco put in. "It's frightening."

"There, you see?" Trent gave Amanda a quick kiss.

"What did you bring me? What did you bring me?" Jenny demanded.

"Talk about mercenary." Laughing, Suzanna scooped her daughter up. When she spotted Sloan in the hallway, her easy smile faded. She tried to tell herself that it was her imagination that his eyes changed whenever he looked at her. It had to be. What possible reason would he have for disliking her on sight?

Sloan studied her another moment, a tall, slender woman with pale blond hair pulled back in a ponytail, a face blessed with classical beauty and sad blue eyes. Dismissing her, he looked back at Trent. His smile came naturally again.

"I hate to interrupt when you're surrounded by beautiful women, but time's wasting."

"Sloan." His arm still around C.C., Trent stepped forward to grip Sloan's hand. In all of his varied groups of acquaintances, associates and colleagues, this was the only man he considered a genuine friend. "On the job already?"

"Getting started."

"You look like you've just gotten back from a long vacation in the tropics instead of six weeks in Budapest. It's good to see you."

"Same here." Sloan sent a quick wink at C.C. "It's really good to see that you're finally developing some taste."

"I like him," C.C. said.

"Women tend to," Trent said. "How's your family?"

Sloan's gaze flicked to Suzanna again. "They're fine."

"You two must have a lot to catch up on." Feeling awkward, Suzanna took her son's hand. "We're going to take a walk before dinner."

Amanda waited until Coco had urged everyone along toward the parlor before she put a hand on Sloan's arm. "Wait."

He grinned at her. "I've been waiting, Calhoun."

She wasn't even tempted to rise to the bait. "I want to know why you look at Suzanna that way."

The humor faded from his eyes. "What way is that?"

"Like you detest her."

It annoyed him that those particular and very private feelings showed so clearly. "You've got more imagination than I gave you credit for."

"It's not my imagination." Baffled, she shook her head. "What could you possibly have against Suzanna? She's the kindest, most good-hearted person I know."

It was difficult not to sneer, but he kept his face bland. "I didn't say I had anything against her. You did."

"You didn't have to say it. Obviously I can't make you talk about it, but—"

"Maybe that's because I'd rather talk about us." Casually he set both hands on the banister behind her, caging her between.

"There is no us."

"Sure there is. There's you and there's me. That makes us. That's real basic grammar."

"If you're trying to change the subject—"

"You're getting that line between your eyebrows again." He lifted a thumb to rub at it. "That Calhoun line. How come you never smile at me the way you smiled at Trent?"

"Because I like Trent."

"It's funny, most people figure I'm an amiable sort of guy."

"Not from where I'm standing."

"Why don't you stand a little closer?"

She had to laugh. If there had been a contest for persistence, Sloan O'Riley would have won hands down. "This is close enough, thanks." More than close enough, she added silently when she had to fight back an urge to run her fingers through that untidy mane of reddish-blond hair. "*Amiable* isn't the word I would use. Now, *cocky, annoying, tenacious,* those might suit."

"I kind of like tenacious." He leaned closer to breathe in her scent. "A man doesn't get very far if he caves in every time he runs into a wall. You climb over, tunnel under, or just knock the whole damn thing down."

She put a hand to his chest before he could close that last inch of distance. "Or he keeps beating his head against it until he has a concussion."

"That's a calculated risk, and worth it if there's a woman behind the wall looking at him the way you look at me."

"I don't look at you any particular way."

"When you forget that you want to be professional, you look at me with those big blue eyes of yours all soft, and a little scared. A lot curious. Makes me want to scoop you up right there and carry you off to some-place real quiet so I can satisfy that curiosity.''

She could imagine it all too clearly, feel it all too sharply. There was only one solution. Escape. ''Well, this has been fun, but I've got to go change.''

''Are you going back to work?''

''No.'' Agile, she swooped under his arm and swung up the steps. ''I've got a date.''

''A date?'' he repeated, but she was already racing across the second floor.

He told himself he wasn't waiting for her, though he'd been pacing the foyer for a good twenty minutes. He wasn't going to hang around like an idiot and watch her go strolling off with some other man—after she'd tied him into knots by just standing there and looking at him. There was plenty for him to do, including en-joying the dinner Coco had invited him to, talking over old times and new plans with Trent, even sitting down at his drawing board. He wasn't about to spend the evening mooning over the fact that some obstinate woman preferred someone else's company to his.

After all, Sloan reminded himself as he paced the foyer, she was free to come and go as she pleased. The same as he was. Neither one of them was branded. Just because he had a hankering for her didn't mean he was going to get riled up when she spent a couple of hours with another man.

The hell it didn't.

Turning, he took the steps two at a time.

''Calhoun?'' He strode down the corridor, banging on doors. ''Damn it, Calhoun, I want to talk to you.''

He was at the far end of the hall and starting back when Amanda opened her door.

"What's going on?" she demanded.

He stared a moment as she stood in the stream of light that spilled out of the room behind her. She'd done something fancy to her hair, he noted, so that it looked sexily rumpled. Played with her face, too, in that damnably sultry way some women have a talent for. Her dress was a pale icy blue, full at the skirt, nipped at the waist with two skinny straps slinking over her shoulders. Chunky stones in a deeper blue glittered at her ears and throat.

She didn't look efficient, he thought furiously. She didn't look competent. She looked as delectable as a pretty white cake on a fancy tray. And he was damned if any other man was going to take even one small nibble.

Her foot was already tapping when he started toward her.

Amiable? she thought, and had to resist the urge to bolt back into her room and lock the door. No one would call him amiable now. He looked as though he'd just finished chewing a mountain of glass and was raring for the second course.

"What kind of date?" he snapped at her, and found himself further incensed by the fact that her skin smelled like glory.

Amanda inclined her head slowly. The hands she had fisted on her hips slid carefully to her sides. When you were facing a raging bull you didn't wave a red flag but tried to ease yourself over the fence. "The usual kind."

"Is that the way you dress for the usual kind?"

Irked, she glanced down and smoothed her skirts. "What's wrong with the way I'm dressed?"

For an answer, he took her arm and swung her around. He'd been right, he thought as his stomach clutched up. Those two little straps were all that were covering her back. Right down to the waist. "Where's the rest of it?"

"Rest of what?"

"The dress."

She turned back, still cautious, and examined his face. "Sloan, I think you've gone around the bend."

She didn't know how right she was, he thought. "I've got as much sense as any man can hang on to after ten minutes with you. Cancel."

"Cancel?" she repeated.

"The date, damn it." He nudged her none too gently toward her bedroom. "Go in and call him up and tell him you can't make it. Ever."

"You really are crazy." She forgot about bulls and red flags and cut loose. "I go where I please and with whom I please. If you think I'm going to break a date with an attractive, charming and intelligent man because some overbearing baboon tells me to, then think again."

"It's the date," he warned, "or that pretty stiff neck of yours."

Her eyes narrowed down to two slits of righteous blue fire. "Don't you threaten me, you pinhead. I have a dinner date with your antithesis. A gentleman." She elbowed him aside. "Now get out of my way."

"I'll get out of your way," he promised. "After I give you something to think about."

He had her back against the wall with his mouth covering hers before she could blink. She could taste the anger. That, she would have fought against to the last breath. But she could also taste the need, and that, she surrendered to. It was such a perfect echo of her own.

He didn't care if it was unreasonable. He didn't care if it was wrong or stupid or any of the other terms that could so easily apply to his actions. He wanted to curse her for making him behave like some reckless teenager. But he could only taste her, drowning in the flavor that he was coming to understand he would always crave. He could only pull her closer against him so that he could feel the instant heat that pumped from her body into his.

He could sense each change as it flowed through her.

First the anger that kept her rigid and aloof. Then the surrender, reluctant then melting so that her bones seemed to dissolve. And the passion overlapping so quickly it stole his breath. It was that he understood he couldn't live without.

Her arms went around him as if they belonged there. Strained against his, her body throbbed until it was one sweet ache. This was an ache that once felt could never be forgotten, would always be craved. Eager, she nipped at his mouth, knowing in another moment delirium could overtake her. Wanting it, wanting that liberating mindless whirl of desire only he could ignite inside her.

Only he.

In one long possessive stroke his hands ran from her shoulders to her wrists, holding there a moment while her pulse scrambled under his palms. When he lifted his head, she leaned back limply against the wall, watching him while she struggled to catch her breath. While she fought to break through the torrent of sensations and understand the feelings beneath them.

The thought of another man touching her, of looking into her face and seeing it flushed with passion as it was now, of seeing her eyes clouded with it, terrified him. Because he preferred good clean anger to fear, he gripped her shoulders again, all but lifting her off her feet.

"Think about that," he told her in a low dangerous voice. "You think about that good and hard."

What had he done to her to make her need so terribly? He had to know, just by looking at her, that he had only to pull her inside her room to take everything he claimed to want. He had only to touch her again to have her desperate to give. He wouldn't even have to ask. It shamed her to realize it, destroyed her to understand that anyone would have such complete power over her pride and her will.

"You made your point," she said unsteadily, infuriated that tears were stinging the back of her eyes and throat. "Do you want to hear me say that you can make me want you? Fine. You can."

The sparkle of tears in her eyes did what her fury couldn't. It beat him soundly. There was regret in his voice when he lifted a hand to her face. "Amanda—"

She stiffened and shut her eyes. If he was gentle—she knew if he showed her even a scrap of tenderness, she would crumble. "You've got your conquest, Sloan. Now I'd appreciate it if you'd let me go."

He let his hand slide to his side before he stepped back. "I'm not going to tell you I'm sorry." But the way she looked at him made him feel as though he had just shattered something small and fragile.

"That's all right. I'm sorry enough for both of us."

"Amanda." Lilah stood at the top of the stairs, watching them both with her sleepy-eyed curiosity. "Your date's here."

"Thanks." Frantic for escape, she turned into her room to grab her jacket and purse. Being careful not to look at Sloan, she hurried out again to rush downstairs. Lilah glanced after her, then walked down the hall to rest her hands on Sloan's shoulders.

"You know, big guy, you look like you could use a friend."

He couldn't begin to put a name to any of the emotions currently running riot through him. "Maybe I'll just go downstairs and throw him out a window."

"You could," Lilah agreed after a moment, "but Mandy's always been a sucker for the underdog."

Sloan swore then decided to work off some of the frustration by pacing the corridor. "So, who is he anyway?"

"I've never met him before. His name's William Livingston."

"And?"

Lilah gave a gentle shrug. "Tall, dark and handsome as the saying goes. Very faint, very charming British accent, Italian suit, upper-class manners. That patina of wealth and breeding without being ostentatious."

Sloan swore and considered punching a hole in the wall. "He sounds just dandy."

"Sounds," she agreed, but her look was troubled.

"What is it?"

"Bad vibes." Absently she ran a hand up and down her arm. "And he had a very muddy aura."

"Give me a break, Lilah."

With a little smile, she glanced back at him. "Don't knock it, Sloan. Remember, I'm on your side. I happen to think you're just what my take-it-all-too-seriously sister needs." In her easy way, she hooked a friendly arm through his. "Relax, Mr. William Livingston doesn't have a chance. Not her type." She laughed as she walked with him to the steps. "She thinks he is, but he's not. So let's go eat. There's nothing like Aunt Coco's Trout Amandine to put you in a good mood."

Pretending she had an appetite, Amanda studied her menu. The restaurant William had chosen was a lovely little place overlooking Frenchman Bay. Since the night was warm, they could enjoy the terrace service with candlelight flickering in the gentle sea breeze, and the fragile scent of spring flowers.

Amanda left the choice of wine up to him and tried to convince herself that she was about to have a delightful evening.

"Are you enjoying Bar Harbor?" she asked.

"Very much. I'm hoping to get some sailing in soon, but in the meantime, I've been content to enjoy the scenery."

"Have you been to the park?"

"Not yet." He glanced over at the bottle the waiter offered, perused the label, then nodded.

"You shouldn't miss it. The view from Cadillac Mountain is stupendous."

"So I'm told." He tasted the wine, approved, then waited for Amanda's to be poured. "Perhaps you'll find some time and act as my guide."

"I don't think—"

"Hotel policy's already been bent," he interrupted, and touched his glass lightly to hers.

"I wanted to ask you how you managed it."

"Very simply. I gave your Mr. Stenerson a choice. Either he could make an exception to his policy, or I could move to another hotel where it wouldn't be an issue."

"I see." She took a thoughtful sip of wine. "That seems a bit drastic just for a dinner."

"A very delightful dinner. I wanted to get to know you better. I hope you don't mind."

What woman could? she asked herself, and only smiled.

It was impossible not to relax, not to be charmed by his stories, flattered by his attentiveness. He did not, as so many successful men did, talk constantly of his business. As an antique dealer he'd traveled all over the world and, throughout the meal, gave Amanda glimpses of Paris and Rome, London and Rio.

When her thoughts drifted now and again to another man, she doubled her determination to enjoy herself where she was, and with whom.

"The rosewood chiffonier in your foyer," he commented as they lingered over coffee and dessert. "It's a beautiful piece."

"Thank you. It's Regency period—I think."

He smiled. "You think correctly. If I had run into it at an auction, I would have considered myself very fortunate."

"My great-grandfather had it shipped over from England when he built the house."

"Ah, the house." William's lips curved as he lifted his cup. "Very imposing. I half expected to see medieval maidens drifting about on the lawn."

"Or bats swooping out of the tower."

On a delighted laugh, he squeezed her hand. "No, but perhaps Rapunzel letting down her hair."

The image appealed and made her smile. "We love it, and always have. Maybe the next time you visit the island you'll stay at The Towers Retreat."

"The Towers Retreat," he murmured, tapping a finger thoughtfully against his lips. "Where have I heard that before?"

"A projected St. James hotel?"

His eyes cleared. "Of course. I read something a few weeks ago. You don't mean to say that your home is The Towers?"

"Yes, it is. We hope to have the retreat ready for occupancy in about a year."

"That is fascinating. But wasn't there some legend attached to the place? Something about ghosts and missing jewelry?"

"The Calhoun emeralds. They were my great-grandmother's."

With a half smile, he tilted his head. "They're real? I thought it was just a clever publicity gimmick. Stay in a haunted house and search for missing treasure. That sort of thing."

"No, in fact we're not at all pleased that the whole business leaked out." Even thinking about it annoyed her so that she began to drum her fingers on the table. "The necklace is real—was real in any event. We don't know where it might have been hidden. In the meantime we're forever bothered by reporters or having to chase erstwhile treasure hunters off the grounds."

"I'm sorry. That's very intrusive."

"We hope to find it soon, and put an end to all the nonsense. Once renovations start, it might turn up under a floorboard."

"Or behind the ubiquitous secret panel," he offered with a smile and made her laugh.

"We don't have any of those—at least that I know of."

"Then your ancestor was remiss. A place like that deserves at least one secret panel." He laid a hand over hers again. "Perhaps you'll let me help you look for it . . . or at least let me use it as an excuse to see you again."

"I'm sorry, but at least for the next few days I'm tied up. My sister's getting married on Saturday."

He smiled over their joined hands. "There's always Sunday. I would like to see you again, Amanda. Very much." He let the subject, and her hand slip gently away.

On the drive home he kept the topics general. No pressure, Amanda thought, grateful. No arrogant assumptions or cocky grins. This was the kind of man who knew how to treat a woman with the proper respect and attention. William wouldn't knock her to the ground and laugh in her face. He wouldn't stalk her down like a gunslinger and fire out demands.

So why was she so let down when they stopped in front of the house and Sloan's car was nowhere in sight? Shaking off the mood, she waited for William to come around and open her door.

"Thank you for tonight," she told him. "It was lovely."

"Yes, it was. And so are you." Very gently he placed his hands on her shoulders before touching his lips to hers. The kiss was very warm, very soft—an expert caress of lips and hands. And to her disappointment, it left her completely unmoved.

"Are you really going to make me wait until Sunday to see you again?"

His eyes told her that he had not been unmoved. Amanda waited for the banked desire in them to strike some chord. But there was nothing.

"William, I—"

"Lunch," he said, adding a charming smile. "Something very casual at the hotel. You can tell me more about the house."

"All right. If I can swing it." She eased away before he could kiss her again. "Thanks again."

"My pleasure, Amanda." He waited, as was proper, for her to go inside. As the door shut behind her, his smile changed ever so slightly, hardened, cooled. "Believe me, it will be my pleasure."

He walked back to his car. He would drive it well out of sight of The Towers. And then he would come back to do a quick and quiet tour of the grounds, to note down the most practical entrances.

If Amanda Calhoun could be his entryway into The Towers, that was all well and good—with the side benefit of romancing a beautiful woman. If she didn't provide him with a way in, he would simply find a different route.

One way or the other, he didn't intend to leave Mount Desert Island without the Calhoun emeralds.

"Did you have a good time?" Suzanna asked when Amanda came in the front door.

"Suze." Amused but not surprised, Amanda shook her head. "You waited up again."

"No, I didn't." To prove it, Suzanna gestured with the mug in her hand. "I just came down to make myself some tea."

Amanda laughed as she walked over to rest her hands on her sister's shoulders. "Why is it that we Irish-as-Paddy's-pig Calhouns can't tell a decent lie?"

Suzanna gave up. "I don't know. We should practice more."

"Honey, you look tired."

"Mmm." Exhausted was the word, but she didn't care for it. Suzanna sipped the tea as they started up the stairs together. "Springtime. Everybody wants their flowers done yesterday. I'm not complaining. It looks like the business is finally going to turn a real profit."

"I still think you should hire on some more help. Between the business and the kids you run yourself ragged."

"Now who's playing mama? Anyway, Island Gardens needs one more good season before I can afford anything but one part-time helper. Plus I like to be busy." Even though fatigue was dragging at her, she paused outside of Amanda's door. "Mandy, can I talk to you for a minute before you go to bed?"

"Sure. Come on in." Amanda left the door slightly ajar as she slipped out of her shoes. "Is something wrong?"

"No. At least nothing I can put my finger on. Can I ask you what you think of Sloan?"

"Think of him?" Stalling, Amanda set her shoes neatly in the closet.

"Impressions, I guess. He seems like a very nice man. Both kids are already crazy about him, and that's an almost foolproof barometer for me."

"He's good with them." Amanda took off her earrings to replace them in her jewelry box.

"I know." Troubled, she wandered the room. "Aunt Coco's set to adopt him. He's slipped right into an easy relationship with Lilah. C.C.'s already fond of him, and not just because he's a friend of Trent's."

Pouting a little, Amanda unclasped her necklace. "His type always gets along beautifully with women."

Distracted, Suzanna merely shook her head. "No, it's not a man-woman kind of thing at all. Just a kind of innate relaxation."

Amanda had no comment for that as she recalled the fevered tension in him a few hours earlier.

"He seems like an easygoing, friendly man."

"But?"

"It's probably my imagination, but whenever he looks at me, I get this wave of hostility." With a half laugh, she shrugged. "Now I sound like Lilah."

Amanda's eyes met her sister's in the mirror. "No, I sensed something myself. I can't explain it. I even called him on it."

"Did he say anything? I don't expect everyone to like me, but when I feel a dislike this strong, at least I want to know why."

"He denied it. I don't know what to say, Suzanna, except that I don't think he's the kind of man who would react that way to someone he doesn't even know." She made a helpless gesture with her hands. "He can certainly be annoying, but I don't think he's a man to be deliberately unfair. Maybe we're both being oversensitive."

"Maybe." Suzanna pushed the uncomfortable feelings away. "We're all a little crazed with C.C.'s wedding, and the renovations. Well, I won't lose any sleep over him." She kissed Amanda's cheek. "Good night."

"Night." As she eased down onto the bed, Amanda let out a long sigh. It was unfortunate, she thought. It was infuriating. But she already knew she'd be losing sleep over him.

Six

She was right on schedule. If there was one thing you could count on about Amanda Calhoun, Sloan thought, it was that she'd be on time. She was moving fast—typically—so he lengthened his stride and crossed the hotel patio to waylay her by the gate leading to the pool. His hand covered hers on the latch.

She jerked away, which was no less than he'd expected. "Don't you have anything better to do?" she asked.

"I want to talk to you."

"This is my time." She shoved open the gate, strode through then whirled around. "My personal time. I don't have to talk to you." To prove it, she slammed the gate smartly in his face.

Sloan took a long, slow breath, then opened the gate. "Okay, you can just listen." He caught up with her as she heaved her towel onto a deck chair.

"I'm not going to talk, and I'm not going to listen. There's absolutely nothing you have to say that could interest me." She stripped off her terry wrap, tossed it aside, then dove into the pool.

Sloan watched her through the first lap. She was mad enough to spit, he thought, then moved his shoulders. So, they'd do it the hard way.

With each kick and stroke, Amanda cursed him. She'd spent half the night replaying their last scene together over and over in her mind. It had made her miserable. It had made her furious. When she'd awakened that morning, she'd promised herself that he would never get the chance to touch her again. Certainly he would never get the chance to make her feel helpless and needy again.

Her life was just beginning to move along as she wanted. There was no way, no way in hell that Sloan O'Riley or anyone else was going to block her path.

She ran straight into him, a dud torpedo into a battleship. Sputtering, she surfaced to see him standing chest high in the water. Bare-chest high.

"What are you doing?"

"I figured I'd have a better chance of getting you to listen in here than I would if I stood on the side and yelled at you."

Eyes narrowed, she slicked the hair back from her face. There was a laugh bubbling in her throat that she refused to acknowledge. "The pool isn't open to guests until ten."

"Yeah, I think you mentioned that. What you didn't mention is that this water is freezing."

"Yeah." Now she did smile, and there was as much humor as smugness in the curve of her lips. "I know. That's why I like to keep moving."

She started off, slicing cleanly through the water. Less than a foot away, he was matching her stroke for stroke. He'd stripped off more than his shirt, she noted. The only thing covering that very long body was a pair of brief navy briefs. Each time her face went into the water, her eyes slid over to take another look.

His broad shoulders and chest tapered down to a narrow waist and hips. The skin was stretched taut over the bones there, without an ounce of excess flesh. His stomach was board flat, and...oh my. When she nearly sucked in water instead of air, Amanda forced her gaze to skip down several strategic inches to the hard, muscled thighs and calves.

The tough, weathered tan was over every inch of exposed flesh. His skin gleamed like wet copper. And what would it feel like to run her hands over it now? To feel those sleek, smooth muscles under her fingers? How could their bodies fit together now, if slick as otters, they slid against each other through the chill water?

Chill? she thought. The pool was beginning to feel like a sauna. Deliberately she pushed off hard and increased her pace. If she could outrace him, maybe she could outrace her own wayward thoughts.

He was still beside her, matching speed and stroke so that they crossed the pool in a kind of unstudied and effortless harmony. It was lovely, almost sensuous, the way their arms lifted and pulled at the same moment, the way their legs scissored and their bodies stretched...like making love, she thought dreamily, then shook herself to knock that hot image from her brain.

Amanda kicked in and put all that frustrated passion into speed. Still, their hands slapped the wall in unison. She began to enjoy it for what it was, an unstated competition between two people who were evenly matched. She'd lost track of the laps and didn't care. When her lungs were straining and her muscles weak, she gripped the edge of the pool to surface, laughing.

He knew she'd never looked more beautiful, with her hair and face drenched with water and her eyes filled with delight. More than anything he'd ever wanted, he wanted to pull her against him then, just to hold her while her laughter danced on the morning air. But he'd made a promise to himself sometime during his own sleepless night. He intended to keep it.

He sent her a friendly grin. "That warmed things up."

"You're pretty good. For an Okie."

"You're not bad yourself, for a female."

She laughed again and rested her head on the side of the pool to look at him. His hair was dark with water, curling over his brow and neck in a way that had her fingers itching to play with it. "I like to race."

"Race? Is that what we were doing? I thought we were just taking a nice, leisurely swim."

She tossed water into his eyes, then stood. "I have to get in."

"Are you going to let me talk to you now?"

The laughter faded from her eyes. "Let's just leave it," she suggested, and hitched herself up on the side of the pool.

He laid a hand on her leg. "Mandy—"

"I don't want to argue with you again. Since we've actually managed to get along for five minutes, why can't we just leave it at that?"

"Because I want to apologize."

"If you'd just—" She broke off to stare at him. "You what?"

"I want to apologize." He stood to put his hands lightly on her arms just beneath her shoulders. "I was out of line last night, way out, and I'm sorry."

"Oh." Disconcerted, she looked down and began to rub at the beads of water on her thigh.

"Now you're supposed to say, all right, Sloan, I accept your apology."

She looked up through wet, spiky lashes, then smiled. Things were suddenly too comfortable to cling to anger. "I guess I do. You acted like such a jerk."

He grimaced. "Thanks a lot."

"You did. Spouting off threats and orders. Then there was all that steam coming out of your ears."

"Want to know why?"

She shook her head and started to rise, but he held her in place. "You brought it up," he pointed out. "I couldn't stand the idea of you being with someone else. Look at me." Gently he cupped her chin, turning her face back to his. "You triggered something in me right off. I can't shake it. I don't much want to."

"I don't think—"

"Thinking has nothing to do with it. I know how I feel when I look at you."

She was losing fast. The quick skip of panic couldn't compete with the flood of pleasure. "I have to think," she murmured. "I'm made that way."

"Okay, well here's something new for you to think about. I'm falling in love with you."

Panic was more than a skip now, but a hard slap. It darted into her eyes as she stared at him. "You don't mean that."

"Yes, I do. And you know it or you wouldn't be sitting there looking like a rabbit caught in the high beams."

"I don't—"

"I'm not asking how you feel," he cut in. "I'm giving you my side of it, so you can get used to it."

She didn't think she would, ever, any more than she would get used to him. Certainly it would be impossible to get used to the feelings shooting off inside her. Is this what love was? she wondered. This edgy and bright sensation that could turn warm and soft without warning? "I don't—I'm not sure how . . ." She let out a huff of breath. "Did you do this just to make me crazy?"

It helped to be able to smile. "Yep. Give me a kiss, Calhoun."

She twisted and slid wetly out of his hold. "I'm not kissing you again, because it erases every intelligent thought from my head."

Now he grinned. "Honey, that's the nicest thing you've ever said to me." When he rose smoothly from the pool, Amanda snatched up her towel. She snapped it once, hard enough to make the air crack.

"Keep back. I mean it. You either give me time to figure all this out or I aim and fire. And I aim below the belt." There was both amusement and challenge in her eyes when she tilted her chin. "You don't have a lot of protection at the moment."

He ran his tongue around his teeth. "You've got me there. How about a drive after you get off work?"

It would be nice, she thought, to go driving with him up into the hills, with the windows open and the air streaming. But, regretfully, duty came first.

"I can't. C.C.'s shower's tonight. We're surprising her when she gets home from work." She frowned a little. "It's on your list."

"Guess it slipped my mind. Tomorrow then."

"I have the final meeting with the photographer, then I have to help Suzanna with the flowers. Not the next night, either," she said before he could ask. "Most of the out-of-town guests will be arriving, plus we've got the rehearsal dinner."

"Then the wedding," he said with a nod. "After the wedding, Calhoun."

"After the wedding, I'll…" She smiled, realizing she was enjoying herself. "I'll let you know." Grabbing her wrap, she headed for the gate.

"Hey. I haven't got a towel."

She tossed a laugh over her shoulder. "I know."

Late that afternoon, Sloan stood out on the lower terrace, making sketches of the exterior of The Towers. He wanted to add another outside stairway without disturbing the integrity of the building. He stopped when Suzanna came out carrying two wicker baskets pregnant with spring flowers.

"I'm sorry." She hesitated, then tried a smile. "I didn't know you were out here. I'm going to set things up for the shower."

"I'll be out of your way in a minute."

"That's all right." She set the basket down and went back inside.

Over the next few minutes, she went back and forth, carrying out chairs and paper decorations. They passed the time in nerve-racking silence until she finally set aside one of Amanda's swans and looked at him.

"Mr. O'Riley, have we met before?"

He kept right on sketching. "No."

"I wondered because you seemed to know me, and have a poor opinion of me."

His gaze lifted coldly to hers. "I don't know you— Mrs. Dumont."

"Then why—" She broke off. She hated confrontations, the way they tightened up her stomach muscles. Turning away, she started back inside. She could feel his eyes on her, icy and resentful. After bracing a hand on the jamb, she forced herself to turn back. "No, I'm not going to do this. You're in my home, Mr. O'Riley, and I refuse to walk on eggshells in my own home ever again. Now I want to know what your problem is."

He tossed his sketch pad onto a small glass-topped table. "The name doesn't ring any bells with you, Mrs. Dumont? O'Riley doesn't strike a chord?"

"No, why should it?"

His mouth tightened. "Maybe if I add a name to it. Megan. Megan O'Riley. Hear any bells now?"

"No." Frustrated, she pushed a hand through her hair. "Will you get to the point?"

"I guess it's easy for someone like you to forget. She wasn't anyone to you but a slight inconvenience."

"Who?"

"Megan. My sister, Megan."

Completely lost, Suzanna shook her head. "I don't know your sister."

The fact that the name meant nothing to her only infuriated him. Sloan stepped toward her, ignoring the quick fear in her eyes. "No, you never met her face-to-face. Why bother? You managed to see that she was pushed aside easily enough. Not that you ended up with any prize. Baxter Dumont was always a bastard, but she loved him."

"Your sister?" Suzanna lifted an unsteady hand to rub at her temple. "Your sister and Bax."

"Starting to get through?" When she started to turn away, he grabbed her arm and whirled her back. "Was it for love or money?" he demanded. "Either way, you could have shown some compassion. Damn it, she was seventeen and pregnant. Couldn't you have stood back far enough to let the spineless sonofabitch see his son?"

She'd gone a translucent shade of white. Under his hand, her arm seemed to turn to water. "Son," she whispered.

"She was just a kid, a terrified kid who'd believed every lie he'd told her. I wanted to kill him, but it would only have made it worse for Meg. But you, you couldn't even find it in your heart to give her the scraps from the table. You went right ahead with your fancy life as if she and the boy didn't exist. And when she called and begged you just to let him see the boy once or twice a year, you called her a whore and threatened to have her son taken away if she ever contacted your precious husband again."

She couldn't get her breath. Not since her last hideous argument with Bax had she found it so difficult to breathe. Weakly she batted at the hand that held her arm. "Please. Please, I need to sit down."

But he was staring at her. As the impetus of his own rage ebbed he could see that it wasn't shame in her eyes, it wasn't derision or even anger. It was pure shock. "My God," he said quietly, "you didn't know."

All she could do was shake her head. When his grip loosened, she turned and bolted into the house. Sloan stood for a moment, pressing his fingers against his eyes. All the disgust he had felt for Suzanna turned sharply on himself. He started after her and ran into a furious Amanda in the doorway.

"What did you do to her?" With both hands she shoved him back. "What the hell did you say to her to make her cry like that?"

The fist in his stomach squeezed tighter. "Where did she go?"

"You're not getting near her again. When I think that I'd begun to believe I could—damn you, O'Riley."

"There's nothing you can say to me that's worse than what I'm already thinking about myself. Now where is she?"

"You go to hell." She slammed the terrace door and flipped the lock.

Sloan gave brief thought to kicking it in then, swearing, went around to the stone steps on the side of the house. He found Suzanna standing on the second-floor balcony, looking out at the cliffs. He'd taken his first step toward her when Amanda burst out of the doors.

"You keep away from her." She already had a protective arm around her sister. "Just turn around and start walking. Don't stop until you get back to Oklahoma."

"This isn't any of your concern," Sloan told her, and Suzanna had to grab hold before Amanda sprang at him.

"It's all right." Suzanna squeezed Amanda's hand. "I need to talk to him, Mandy. Alone."

"But—"

"Please. It's important. Go down and finish setting up, will you?"

Reluctant, Amanda stepped back. "If it's what you want." She aimed a killing look at Sloan. "Watch your step."

When they were alone, Sloan struggled for the right words. "Mrs. Dumont. Suzanna—"

"What's his name?" she asked.

"What?"

"The boy. What's his name?"

"I don't—"

"Damn it, what's his name?" She whirled away from the wall. Shock had been replaced by angry tears. "He's half brother to my children. I want to know his name."

"Kevin. Kevin O'Riley."

"How old is he?"

"Seven."

Turning back to the sea, she shut her eyes. Seven years before she had been a new bride, full of hope and dreams and blind love. "And Baxter knew? He knew that she'd had his child?"

"Yes, he knew. Megan wouldn't tell anyone at first who the father was. But after she'd called and spoken to you . . . but she didn't speak to you, did she?"

"No." Suzanna continued to stare straight ahead. "Baxter's mother perhaps."

"I want to apologize."

"There's no need. If it had been one of my sisters, I would have struck out with more than a few hard words." To warm herself she cupped her elbows with her hands. "Go on."

She was tougher than she looked, Sloan thought, but it didn't ease his conscience. "After she'd called, she fell apart. That's when she finally told me everything. How she'd met Dumont when she'd gone to New York to visit some friends. He was there on some business and he started showing her around. She'd never been to New York before, and it—and he dazzled her. She was just a kid."

"Seventeen," Suzanna murmured.

"And naive with it. Well, she got over that quick enough." The bitterness came though. "He gave her all the usual bull about getting married, about how he'd come out to Oklahoma and meet her family. Once she got home, he never contacted her. She got through to him on the phone once or twice. He made excuses and more promises. Then she found out she was pregnant."

He steadied himself, trying not to remember how angry and frightened he'd been when he'd learned his baby sister was going to have a baby of her own.

"When she told him, he changed tactics fast. He said some pretty awful things to her, and she grew up fast. Too fast."

Suzanna understood that, more than he could know. "It must have been terribly difficult for her, having the child without having the father."

"She handled herself. I have a very supportive family. Well, you'd know about that."

"Yes."

"Luckily, money wasn't a problem, either, so she could get all the care she and the baby needed. She never wanted his money, Suzanna."

"No, I understand that, too."

He nodded slowly, seeing that she did. "And when Kevin was born . . . well, Meg was great. It was for his sake that she tried to contact Dumont again, and eventually decided to appeal to his wife. All she wanted was for her son to have some contact with his father."

"I understand." Steadier, she turned around to look at him. "Sloan, if I had any influence with Bax I'd use it." She lifted her hands and let them fall. "But I don't, not even when it concerns the children he's chosen to acknowledge."

"I figure Kevin's better off the way things are. Suzanna—" he dragged a hand through his disordered hair "—how the hell did a woman like you end up with Dumont?"

She smiled a little. "Once I was a young, naive girl who believed in happy ever after."

He wanted to take her hand but wasn't certain she'd accept it. "I know you said you didn't want an apology, but I'd feel a hell of a lot better if you'd take it just the same."

It was she who offered her hand. "It's easy to do when it's family. I guess in an odd way, that's what we are." She pressed her free hand to their joined ones. Later, she promised herself, she would find a few minutes alone to let the grief come. And to let it go. "I want to ask you a favor. I'd like for my children to know about Kevin, and unless it would upset your sister, for them to have a chance to meet each other."

"When I take a wrong turn, I take it big. It would mean a lot to her."

"Jenny and Alex are going to be thrilled." She looked at her watch. "Speaking of which, they're probably already home from school and driving Aunt Coco crazy. I'd better go."

He looked down the steps toward the terrace. And thought of Amanda. "Me, too. I've got other fences to mend."

Suzanna lifted a brow. "Good luck."

He had a feeling he was going to need it. By the time he'd reached the terrace, he was sure of it. Amanda was there, fastening streamers while Lilah leisurely tied balloons to the back of chairs. A long table was already covered with a frilly white cloth.

Amanda heard the scrape of boot heels on stone and turned to aim one deadly glare. Lilah didn't need another hint.

"Well." She flicked a balloon with a fingertip to send it dancing. "I think I'll go see if Aunt Coco's got any of those chocolate pastries ready." As she walked by Sloan, she paused. Unlike Amanda's, her eyes were cool, but the meaning was clear. "I'd hate to think I was wrong about you." She walked through the terrace doors and, after a brief hesitation, shut them to give her sister privacy.

Amanda didn't wait to pounce. "You've got a nerve, or maybe you're just plain stupid, showing your face here after what you did."

"You don't know anything about it. Suzanna and I worked it out."

"Oh, you think so?" Ready to joust, she slammed down a package of pretty pink-and-silver plates. "Not by a long shot. When I think that just a few hours ago you'd nearly convinced me you were the kind of man I could care about, then I come home and find my sister running away from you looking devastated. I want to know what you did."

"I ran with the wrong information. And I'm sorry about it."

"That's not good enough."

His own emotions were a bit too raw for reason. "Well, it's going to have to be. If you want to know more, you're just going to have to ask Suzanna."

"I'm asking you."

"And I'm telling you that what happened was between her and me. It doesn't have anything to do with you."

"That's where you're wrong." She crossed the terrace until they were toe to toe. "You mess with one Calhoun, you mess with them all. I may have to put up with you until after the wedding, since you're supposed to be best man. But when it's over, I'm going to do whatever I have to do to see to it that you go back where you came from."

Pushed to the end of his chain, he took her by the lapels. "I told you before, I finish what I start."

"You are finished, O'Riley. The Towers doesn't need you, and neither do I."

He was just about to prove her wrong when Trent opened the terrace doors. Trent took one look at his friend and future sister-in-law glaring daggers at each other and cleared his throat.

"Looks like I'm going to have to work on my timing."

"Your timing's perfect." Amanda rammed an elbow into Sloan's stomach before she pulled away. "We've got no time for men around here tonight. Why don't you take this jerk you've sicced on us and go do something manly." She shoved by Trent and stalked into the house.

"Well." Trent let out a long breath. "I don't think I mentioned the Calhoun temperament when I asked you to take on the job."

"No, you didn't." Scowling at the empty doorway, Sloan rubbed his stomach. "Is there a dark, noisy bar anywhere in this town?"

"I guess we could find one."

"Good. Let's go get drunk."

He found the bar, and he found the bottle. Sloan slumped in the corner booth and hissed through his teeth as the whiskey stung his throat. Over the first drink, and the second, he told Trent about his altercation with Suzanna.

"Baxter Dumont is Kevin's father? You never told me."

"I gave Meg my word I wouldn't tell anybody. Even our folks don't know."

Trent was silent a moment, sipping thoughtfully at his club soda. "It's hard to figure out how such a selfish bastard managed to father three terrific kids."

"It's a puzzle, all right." Sloan signaled for another round. "Then I go off and unload both barrels on Suzanna." He broke off and swore. "Damn it, Trent, I'm never going to forget the way she looked when I cut loose on her."

"She'll handle it. From what C.C.'s told me, she's dealt with worse."

"Yeah, maybe. Maybe. But I don't care much for slapping down women. I was already feeling like something you scrape off your shoe when Amanda lit into me."

"These women stick together."

"Yeah." Scowling, Sloan drank again. "Like a dirt clod."

"Why didn't you explain things to her?"

Sloan shrugged and knocked back more whiskey. He had his own share of pride. "It wasn't any of her business."

"You just explained it to me."

"That's different."

"Okay. Do you want some pretzels to go with that?"

"No."

They sat for a moment, nursing drinks, two dynamically different men, one in battered jeans, the other in tailored slacks; one slumped comfortably, the other comfortably alert. They'd both come from money— Trent from real estate, Sloan from oil, but their backgrounds and family lives had been opposites. Trent's first experience with real family ties had come through the Calhouns, and Sloan had known them always. They had almost nothing in common, and yet in their first semester in college they had become friends and had remained so for more than ten years.

Because he was feeling sorry for himself, Sloan enjoyed the sensation of getting steadily drunk. Because he recognized the symptoms, Trent stayed meticulously sober.

Over yet another drink, Sloan eyed his friend. "When'd you start wearing basketball shoes?"

Trent glanced down at his own feet and grinned to himself. They were a symbol of sorts of the way one hot-tempered brunette had changed his life. "They're not basketball shoes, they're running shoes."

"What's the difference?" Sloan narrowed his eyes. "And you're not wearing a tie. How come you're not wearing a tie?"

"Because I'm in love."

"Yeah." With a short oath, Sloan sat back. "See what it's doing to you? It makes you nuts."

"You hate ties."

"Exactly. Damn woman's been driving me crazy since the first time I saw her."

"C.C.?"

"No, damn it. We were talking about Amanda."

"Right." Settling back in the seat, Trent smiled. "Well, some woman's always driving you crazy. I've never seen anyone with a more . . . admirable affection for the gentler sex."

"Gentler my ass. First she runs into me, then she knocks me on my butt. I can hardly say two words without having her claw at me." After calling for another drink, he leaned across the table. "You've known me for over ten years. Wouldn't y'say that I was a kind of even-tempered, affable sort of man?"

"Absolutely." Trent grinned. "Except when you're not."

Sloan slapped a hand on the table. "There you go." Nodding agreement, he pulled out a cigar. "So what the hell's wrong with her?"

"You tell me."

"I'll tell you." He jabbed the cigar toward Trent's face. "She's got the devil's own temper and a mule's stubbornness to go with it. If a man can keep his eyes off her legs, it's plain enough to see." He picked up his fresh whiskey and scowled into it. "She sure enough has first-class legs."

"I've noticed. They run in the family." As Sloan downed the liquor, Trent winced. "Am I going to have to carry you home?"

"More'n likely." He settled back to let the whiskey spin in his head. "What you want to go and get yourself married for, Trent? We'd both be better off hightailing it outta here."

"Because I love her."

"Yeah." On a sigh, Sloan let out a lazy stream of smoke. "That's how they get you. They get you all tangled up so you can't think straight. Used to be I thought women were God's own pleasure, but I know better now. They've only got one reason for being here, and that's to make a man's life misery." He squinted over at Trent. "Have you seen the way her skirt jiggles when she walks—especially when she's in a hurry, like she always is."

On a chuckle, Trent lifted his glass again. "I take the Fifth on that one."

"And the sassy way her hair moves when she's yelling at you. Her eyes get all snappy. Then you grab ahold of her to shut her up, and God Almighty." He took another quick slug of whiskey, but it did nothing to put out the fire. "You ever missed your step and gone down on an electric fence?"

"Can't say I have."

"It burns," Sloan murmured. "Burns like fire and knocks you senseless for a minute. When you get your senses back, you're kind of numb and shaky."

Carefully Trent set down his drink and leaned closer to study his friend. "Sloan, is this leading where I think it's leading, or are you just drunk?"

"Not drunk enough." Annoyed, he shoved the glass aside. "I haven't had a decent night's sleep since I set eyes on her. And since I set eyes on her it's like there was never anyone else. Like there's never going to be anyone else." With his elbows propped on the table, he rubbed his hands over his face. "I'm crazy in love with her, Trent, and if I could get my hands on her right now, I'd strangle her."

"Calhoun women have a talent for that." He grinned at Sloan. "Welcome to the club."

It rained all day so I could not go down to the cliffs to see Christian. For most of the morning I played games with the children to keep them from becoming fussy about being kept indoors. They squabbled, of course, but Nanny distracted them with cookies. Even the boys enjoyed the tea party we had with Colleen's little china dishes. For me, it was one of those sweet, insular days that a mother always remembers—the way her children laugh, the funny questions they ask, the way they lay their heads on your lap when nap time approaches.

The memory of this single day is as precious to me as any I have had, or will have. They will not be my babies very long. Already Colleen is talking about balls and dresses.

It makes me wonder what my life would be like if it could be Christian who would stroll into the parlor. He would not nod absently as he opened the brandy decanter. He would not forget to ask about his children.

No, my Christian would come to me first, his hands outstretched to meet mine as I rose to kiss him. He would laugh, as I hear him laugh during our stolen hours at the cliff.

And I would be happy. Without this bittersweet pain in my heart. Without this guilt. There would be no need then for me to seek the quiet and solitude of my tower, or to sit alone watching the gray rain as I write my dreams in this book.

I would be living my dreams.

But it is all just a fancy, like one of the stories I tell the children at bedtime. A happy-ever-after story with handsome princes and beautiful maidens. My life is not a fairy tale. But perhaps, someday someone will open these pages and read my story. I hope they will have a kind and generous heart, condemn me not for my disloyalty to a husband I have never loved, but rejoice for me in my joy in those few short hours with a man I will love even after death.

Seven

Sloan's head was filled with tiny little men wielding pick axes. To quiet them, he tried rolling over. A definite mistake, he realized, as the slight movement sent a signal to the army-navy band waiting in the wings to punch up the percussions. Gingerly he pulled a pillow over his face, hoping to smother the sound or—if that didn't work—himself.

But the noise kept booming until his abused system told him it was the door, not just the hangover. Giving up, he stumbled out of bed, grateful there was no one around to hear him whimper. With the road gang working away inside his temples, he turned the air between the bedroom and the parlor door a ribald shade of blue.

When he wrenched it open, Amanda took one look, noting the bloodshot eyes, night stubble and curled lip.

He was wearing the jeans, unclasped, that he'd fallen asleep in, and nothing else.

"Well," she said primly, "you look like you had a delightful time last night."

And she looked as neat and crisp as a freshly starched shirt. It was, he was sure, reason enough for homicide. "If you came up here to ruin my day, you're too late." He started to swing the door shut, but she held it open and stepped inside.

"I have something to say to you."

"You've said it." Instantly he regretted turning sharply away. As his head throbbed nastily, he vowed to hold on to what was left of his dignity. He would not crawl away, but walk.

Because he looked so pitiful, she decided to help him out. "I guess you feel pretty lousy."

"Lousy?" He narrowed his eyes to keep them from dropping out of his head. "No, I feel dandy. Just dandy. I live for hangovers."

"What you need is a cold shower, a couple of aspirin and a decent breakfast."

After making an inarticulate sound in his throat, he groped his way toward the bedroom. "Calhoun, you're on dangerous ground."

"I won't be in your way long." Determined to accomplish her mission, she followed him. "I just want to talk to you about—" She broke off when he slammed the bathroom door in her face. "Well." Blowing out a huffy breath, she set her hands on her hips.

Inside, Sloan stripped off his jeans then stepped into the shower. With one hand braced on the tile, he turned the water on full cold. His single vicious curse bounced along the walls then slammed right back into his head.

Still, he was a little steadier when he stepped out again, fought with the cap on the aspirin bottle and downed three.

His hangover hadn't gone away, he thought, but at least he was now fully awake to enjoy it. Wrapping a towel around his waist, he walked back into the parlor.

He'd thought she would have gotten the message, but there she was, hunched over his drawing board with glasses perched on her nose. She'd tidied up, too, he noted, emptying ashtrays, piling cups on the room service tray, picking up discarded clothes. In fact, she had her hands full of his clothes while she studied his drawings.

"What the hell are you doing?"

She glanced up and, determined to be cheerful, smiled. "Oh, you're back." The sight of him in nothing but a damp towel had her careful to keep her eyes strictly on his face. "I was just taking a look at your work."

"I don't mean that, I mean what are you doing picking up after me? It's not part of your job to play Sally Domestic."

"I didn't see how you could work in a sty," she shot back, "so I straightened up a little while I was waiting for you."

"I like working in a sty. If I didn't, I would've picked the damn stuff up myself."

"Fine." Incensed, she hurled his clothes into the air so that they scattered over the room. "Better?"

Slowly he pulled off the T-shirt that had landed on his head. "Calhoun, do you know what's more dangerous than a man with a hangover?"

"No."

"Nothing." He took one measured step toward her when there was another knock at the door.

"That's your breakfast." Amanda's voice was clipped as she strode toward the door. "I had them put a rush on it."

Defeated, Sloan sank onto the couch and put his head in his hands so that he could catch it easily when it fell off. "I don't want any damn breakfast."

"Well, you'll eat it and stop feeling sorry for yourself." She signed the check, then took the tray herself to place it on the table in front of him. "Whole wheat toast, black coffee and a Virgin Mary, heavy on the hot sauce. It'll take the edge off."

"An electric planer couldn't take the edge off." But he reached for the coffee.

Satisfied that she had made a good start, Amanda took off her glasses and slipped them into her pocket. He really did look pathetic, she thought. His wet hair was dripping down his face. She had a strong urge to kneel down beside him and stroke those damp curls back. But he'd probably have snapped her hand off at the wrist, and she had an equally strong urge to survive.

"Trent mentioned that you did quite a bit of drinking last night."

After trying the spiced-up tomato juice, he eyed her narrowly. "So you came by to see the morning-after in person."

"Not exactly." Her fingers toyed with her name tag, then the top button on her jacket. "I thought since it was my fault you got into this condition, I should—"

"Hold it. If I get drunk, it's because my hand reaches for the bottle."

"Yes, but—"

"I don't want your sympathy, Calhoun, or your guilt any more than I want your maid service."

"Fine." Pride and temper went to war. Pride won. "I merely came by this morning to apologize."

He bit off another piece of toast. It did soothing things to the rocky sea of his belly. "What for?"

"For what I said, and the way I acted yesterday." Unable to stand still, she walked over to the window and pulled the shades open, ignoring Sloan's quick hiss of pain. "Although I still think I was perfectly justified. After all, I only knew that you'd said something to hurt Suzanna badly." But there was regret in her eyes when she turned back. "When she told me about your sister—about Bax—I realized how you must have been feeling. Damn it, Sloan, you could have told me yourself."

"Maybe. Maybe you could have trusted me."

She took her glasses out again, playing with the earpieces to keep her hands busy. "It wasn't really a matter of trust, but of automatic reflex. You don't know what Suzanna went through, how deeply she was hurt. Or if you do, because of your own sister, then you should understand why I couldn't bear to see her look like that again." She shoved the glasses away. When she looked at him, her eyes were damp. "And it was worse, because I have feelings for you."

If there was one thing he had no defense against, it was tears. Wanting to ward them off as much as he wanted to make peace, he rose to take her hands. "I made my share of mistakes yesterday." Smiling, he rubbed her knuckles over his cheek. It felt good— damn good. "I guess it's as hard for you to apologize as it is for me."

"If you mean it's like swallowing a lump of coal, then you're right."

"Why don't we call it even, all around?" But when he lowered his head to kiss her, she stepped back.

"I really need to think straight for a while."

He caught her hand again. "I really need to make love with you."

Her heart took a quick leap into her throat. For someone who moved so slowly, how did he get from one point to the next so fast? "I'm, ah, on duty. I'm already over my break, and Stenerson—"

"Why don't I give him a call?" Still smiling, he began to kiss her fingers. The hangover was down to a dull ache, not nearly as noticeable as another, more pleasant one in the pit of his stomach. "Tell him I need the assistant manager for a couple hours."

"I think—"

"There you go again," he murmured, brushing his lips lightly over hers.

"No, really, I have to..." Her mind clouded as he trailed those lips down her throat. "I really have to get back to my desk. And I—" She took a big, shuddering gasp of air. "I need to be sure." Scrambling for survival, she pulled away. "I have to know what I'm doing."

Sloan pressed a hand to the familiar burn that spread inside his gut. He had a feeling he was just going to have to live with it for a while longer. "Tell you what, Calhoun. You think about it, and think hard, until after the wedding. Like we said before." Before she could relax, he had her chin cupped firmly in his hand. "And after the wedding, if you don't come to me, you'd better run fast."

The line appeared between her brows. "That sounds like an ultimatum."

"No, that's a fact. If I were you, I'd get out that door now, while I still had the chance."

All dignity, she marched to it before turning back with a smile that should have tipped him off. "Enjoy your breakfast," she told him, then slammed the door with a vengeance. She could almost see him holding his battered head.

"I didn't think I'd be nervous." C.C. stared at the wedding dress of snowy silk and lace that hung on the back of her closet door. "Maybe it'd be better if I just wore regular clothes."

"Don't be ridiculous. And stop fidgeting." Amanda bent close to her sister to add a bit more blusher to her cheeks. "You're supposed to be nervous."

"Why?" Annoyed with herself, C.C. pressed a hand to her fluttery stomach. "I love Trent and want to get married. Why should I be nervous now that it's going to happen?" She looked back at the dress and swallowed. "Less than an hour from now."

Amanda grinned. "Maybe I should call Aunt Coco and have her give you a booster-shot course on the birds and the bees."

"Very funny." But the idea did amuse her enough to make her smile. "When's Suzanna coming back?"

"I told you, as soon as she has the kids dressed. Jenny might love the idea of being flower girl, but Alex is a most reluctant ring bearer. He'd rather be carrying a machine gun down the aisle than a satin pillow. And before you ask, again, Lilah is supposed to be downstairs making sure all the last-minute details go off properly. Though why we think we can trust her is beyond me.''

"She'll be fine. She always handles things when it's important.'' C.C. laid a hand on Amanda's. "And it is important, Mandy.''

"I know, honey. It's the most important day of your life.'' Misty-eyed, she laid her cheek against C.C.'s. "Oh, I feel as though I should say something profound, but I can only say be happy.''

"I will be, and it's not as if I'll be really going away. We'll be living here most of the time, except when . . . when we're in Boston.'' Her throat filled up.

"Don't start,'' Amanda warned. "I mean it. After all the work I put in making you beautiful, you're not going out in the garden with red eyes and a runny nose.'' Blowing her own, she stepped back. "Now, let me help you get dressed.''

When Suzanna came in a short time later, a child's hand in each of hers, she had to struggle with her own tears. "Oh, C.C., you look wonderful.''

"Are you sure?'' Fretting, she plucked at the lace at her throat. The dress was a slim column, elegantly simple with only that whisper of lace at the neck, and another whisper at the hem to adorn it. "Maybe I should have gone for something less formal.''

"No, it's perfect.'' Suzanna bent down to her son, her own dress rustling with the movement. "Alex, stand still for five minutes, please.''

He tried out the sneer he'd been practicing in the mirror. "I hate cummerbunds.''

"I know, but if you don't want me to strap it around your mouth, you'll stand still.'' Tweaking his nose, she straightened. "I have something for you.'' She offered

C.C. a small box. Inside was a single teardrop sapphire on a braided gold chain.

"Mama's necklace," C.C. whispered.

"Aunt Coco gave it to me when I—on my wedding day." She took it out to fasten around her sister's neck. "I want you to have it and wear it on yours."

C.C. lifted a hand to it, closing her fingers around the stone. "I'm not nervous anymore."

"Then that's my cue to panic." Afraid to say more, Amanda gave her a quick kiss. "I'll run downstairs and make sure everything's on schedule."

"Mandy—"

Amanda smiled over her shoulder. "Yes, I'll send Lilah up." She went out, hurrying downstairs while she ticked off duties in her mind. Taking a moment, she stopped by the hall mirror to adjust the spray of baby's breath over her ear.

"You look great." She glanced over and saw Sloan. "Just great."

"Thanks." They stood awkwardly a moment, a man in a tuxedo and a woman in a tea-length gown the color of ripe peaches. "I, uh, where's Trent?"

"He needed a couple of minutes to himself. His father came by with some advice." Relaxing slowly, Sloan grinned. "When a man's been married as many times as Mr. S.J., he comes up with some interesting viewpoints." He had to laugh at the expression on Amanda's face. "Don't worry, I nudged him along outside with a glass of champagne and Coco. Seems like they're old friends."

"I think she met him a long time ago." When Sloan took a step toward her, she began to talk rapidly. "You look terrific. I didn't expect you to look good in a tuxedo." Before he'd finished laughing, she was rambling on. "What I mean is I didn't expect it to suit you. I mean—"

"You're cute when you're flustered."

She ended up smiling at him. As far as she could recall, he was the only person who had ever accused her of being cute. "I really have to go." Before she gave in to the urge to fuss with his tie or something equally mushy. "We'll be starting in a few minutes. Guests need to be seen to."

"Most everybody's already in the garden."

"The photographer."

"All set up."

"The champagne."

"On ice." He took the last step toward her and tilted up her chin with a fingertip. "Weddings make you nervous, Calhoun?"

"This one does."

"Going to save a dance for me?"

"Of course."

He toyed with the flowers in her hair. "And later?"

"I . . ."

"C.C.'s ready!" Alex bellowed from the top of the stairs. "Can we get this dumb thing over with."

With a laugh, Sloan kissed her fingers. "Don't worry, I'll make sure the groom's in place."

"All right, and—damn!" She swore, then snatched up the ringing phone. "Hello? Oh, William, I really can't talk. We're about to start the wedding. . . . Tomorrow?" She lifted a distracted hand to her hair. "No, of course. Umm . . . yes, that's fine. Late afternoon would be best. Three o'clock? I'll see you then." Still off balance, she turned to find Sloan watching her with very cool, measuring green eyes.

"You take big chances, Calhoun."

"That wasn't what it sounded like." She caught herself trying to explain and frowned. "What do you mean, 'chances'?"

"That's something we'd better discuss later. We've got a wedding to get to."

"You're absolutely right." They strode off in opposite directions.

Moments later, the Calhoun women took their turns walking down the garden path. First Suzanna, then Lilah, then Amanda, followed by a beaming Jenny and a thoroughly embarrassed Alex. They took their places with Amanda doing her best not to glance in Sloan's direction. Then she forgot everything as she watched C.C. come forward, a wispy veil over her hair. Beside her, prepared to give her youngest niece away, Coco held her arm and wept.

She watched her sister marry under an arbor of delicately fragrant wisteria. Through a mist of tears she looked on as the man who was now her brother-in-law slipped the circle of emeralds onto C.C.'s finger. The look that passed between them spoke more eloquently of promises than any of the vows exchanged. With her hands clasped with her sisters', she saw C.C.'s face lift to Trent's as they shared their first kiss as husband and wife.

"Is it finally over?" Alex wanted to know.

"No," Amanda heard herself say as her gaze drifted to Sloan's. "It's just beginning."

"Beautiful wedding." After Amanda was thoroughly kissed by Trent's father, she managed to nod in agreement. "Trent tells me you put most of it together."

"I'm good with details," she said, and offered him a plate for the buffet.

"So I hear." Trim, tanned and expansive, St. James smiled at her. "I've also heard that all of the Calhoun sisters are lovely. I can now corroborate that myself."

He was quite the elegant old flirt, Amanda mused but smiled back as he arranged food on his plate. "We're delighted to welcome you to the family."

"It's odd the way things have worked out," he said. "A year ago I looked up from my boat in the bay and saw this house. I simply had to have it. Now, not only is part of it a portion of my business, but it's a part of my family." He glanced over to see Trent and C.C. dancing on the terrace. "She's made him happy," he said quietly. "I never quite had the knack for that myself." With a vague movement of his shoulders, he brushed the thought aside. "Would you care to dance?"

"I'd love to."

They'd hardly taken three steps on the dance floor, when Sloan swung Coco around and smoothly switched partners.

"You might have asked," Amanda muttered as his arms slid around her.

"I did, before. Anyway, she'll flirt with him the way he wants instead of treating him like a distant relation."

"He is a distant relation." But she glanced over and saw that Coco already had St. James laughing. "Everything's going well, I think."

"Smooth as glass." Just as smoothly, he noted, as she fit into his arms. "You did a good job."

"Thanks, but I hope it's the last wedding I have to plan for quite a while."

"Don't you think about getting married yourself?"

She missed a step and nearly stumbled over his feet. "No—that is, yes, but not really."

"That's a definitive answer."

"What I mean is it's not in my short-range plans." No matter what longings had tugged at her when her gaze had locked with Sloan's under the arbor. "I'm going to be busy over the next few years with the retreat. I've always wanted to manage a first-class hotel, to make policy instead of just carrying it out. It's what I've been working for, and now that Trent's giving me the chance, I can't afford to divide my loyalties."

"An interesting way of seeing it. With me it's always been a matter of getting tied down with one person in one place, then finding out I made a mistake."

"There's that, too." Relieved that they weren't arguing, she smiled. "I never asked, but I guess you do a lot of traveling."

"Here and there. A drawing board's portable. You might like to do some traveling yourself, check out the hotel competition. Why don't we go somewhere quiet and talk about it?"

"Sorry, I'm on call. And if you want to be helpful, you'll play best man and go get a few more bottles of champagne from the kitchen." She tucked her arm through his. "I've got to run up and get the streamers anyway."

"Streamers?"

"To decorate the car. They're up in my room."

"Tell you what," Sloan began when they reached the kitchen. "Why don't I come up to your room and help you get the streamers?"

"Because I want to decorate the car before they get back from their honeymoon." With a laugh, she dashed away. Amanda was halfway down the hall on the second floor when the creak of a board overhead had her stopping. Tuned to the moans and groans of the old house, she frowned. Footsteps, she realized. Definitely footsteps. Wondering if one of the wedding guests had decided to take an impromptu tour, she started back toward the stairway. On the third-floor landing, she spotted Fred, curled up and sleeping.

"Fine watchdog," she muttered, bending down to shake him. He only rolled over with a groggy snore. "Fred?" Alarmed, she shook him again, but instead of bouncing up, ready to play, he lay still. When she picked him up, his head lolled onto her hand. Even as she gathered him up, someone shoved her from behind and sent her headfirst into the wall.

Stunned and sprawled on the dog, she struggled up to her knees. Someone was running down the stairs. With the wrath of the Calhouns filling her, she jumped up, Fred tucked under her arm like a furry football, and gave chase. She turned sharply on the second-floor landing, ears straining. On an oath she headed down to the main floor, heels clattering on wood. Sloan caught her as she stumbled on the last step.

"Whoa. What's the hurry?" Grinning, he scanned her tumbled hair and the spray of baby's breath now hanging to her shoulder. "What did you do, Calhoun, trip over the dog?"

"Did you see him?" she demanded, and broke out of Sloan's hold to rush to the door.

"See who?"

"There was somebody upstairs." Her heart was pumping fast and hard. She hadn't noticed it before. Or the fact that her legs were shaky. "Someone was sneaking around on the third floor. I don't know what they did to Fred."

"Hold on." Gently now, he guided her back to the stairs and eased her down. "Let's have a look." He took the dog, then pulling up an eyelid, swore. When he looked back at Amanda, there was a flat grimness in his eyes she'd never seen before. "Somebody drugged him."

"Drugged him?" Amanda gathered Fred back to her breast. "Who would drug a poor little dog?"

"Someone who didn't want him to bark, I imagine. Tell me what happened."

"I heard someone on the third floor and went up to see. I found Fred, just lying there." She nuzzled the puppy. "When I started to pick him up, someone pushed me into the wall."

"Are you hurt?" His hands were instantly on her face.

"No." She let out a disgusted breath. "If it hadn't stunned me for a minute, I would have caught him."

Eyes narrowed, Sloan sat back on his heels. "Didn't it occur to you to call for help?"

"No." The baby's breath was tickling her shoulder, so she pulled it away.

"Idiot."

"Look, O'Riley, nobody's going to poke around in my house, and hurt my dog and get away with it. If he hadn't had a start on me, I'd have caught him."

"And then what?" he demanded. "God Almighty, Amanda, don't you realize he would have given you more than a push."

Actually she hadn't thought of it. But that didn't change the bottom line. "I can take care of myself. It's bad enough when people come to the door, or sneak around the grounds, but when they start breaking into the house, they're going to answer for it." She gave a nod of satisfaction as she rose. "I scared him good, anyway. The way he was running, he's halfway to the village by now. I don't think he'll be coming back. What about Fred?"

"I'll take care of him." He took the sleeping puppy from her. "He just needs to sleep it off. And you need to call the police."

"After the wedding." She shook her head before he could object. "I'm not spoiling this for C.C. and Trent just because some jerk decided to do some treasure hunting. What I will do is check the third floor and see if anything's missing. Then I'm going to go back out and make sure everything runs smoothly until it's time to throw rice at the bride and groom. After that, I'll call the police."

"Got it all figured out, nice and tidy, as usual." The hot edge of his temper seeped into his voice. "Things don't always work that way."

"I'll make it work."

"Sure you will. Can't have something like attempted robbery and a little assault mess up all your short-term plans. Just like you can't have someone like me messing up your long-term ones."

"I don't see what you're so upset about."

"You wouldn't," he said tightly. "You hear somebody in the house where they shouldn't be, get hit in the head, but you don't even think about calling for me. You don't think about asking somebody for help, not even when that somebody's in love with you."

The tightness in her chest returned, making her voice clipped. "I was just doing what I had to do."

"Yeah," he agreed with a slow nod. "You go ahead and do what you have to do now. I'll get out of your way."

Eight

And he'd stay out of her way, Sloan promised himself. The woman had fuddled his brain long enough.

He stood out on the terrace off his bedroom, trying to enjoy the balmy May evening. He'd left The Towers as soon as it had been possible. Oh, he'd done his duty, he thought. Amanda wasn't the only one who could do what was expected of her. With the help of Suzanna and the children, he'd decorated the newlyweds' car. A smile plastered on his face, he'd tossed the rice. He'd even given Coco his handkerchief when her own proved inadequate for her happy tears. He'd waited with a worried Lilah until Fred had given his first groggy bark.

Then he'd gotten the hell out of there.

She didn't need him. The fact that he hadn't realized until now just how much he needed her to need him didn't make it any easier. Here he was, waiting to sweep her off her feet, and she was chasing after thieves or making dates with guys named William. Well, he was through making a fool of himself over her.

She had a job to do, and so did he. She had a life to live, and so did he. It was time he put things back in perspective. A man had to be crazy to think about saddling himself with an ornery, my-way-or-nothing female. A sane man wanted a nice, calm woman who'd give him some peace after a long day, not one who riled him up every time he took a breath.

So, he'd put Amanda Calhoun out of his mind and be a happier man for it.

"Sloan."

With one hand still braced on the railing, he turned. She was in the doorway, her fingers linked tight together. She'd changed the silk dress for a crisp cotton blouse and slacks. Very streamlined, very simple and certainly not sexy enough to make his heart start jumping as it was now.

"I knocked," she began, then with an uneasy movement of her shoulders, stepped onto the terrace. "I was afraid you wouldn't let me in, so I got a pass key."

"Isn't that against the rules?"

"Yes. I'm sorry, but I couldn't talk to you at home. I didn't even think I wanted to. Then after the police came and went, and everything was as close to normal as it gets, I couldn't settle down." She let out a long breath. Obviously he wasn't going to say anything to make it easier. He was just going to stand there, his white dress shirt unbuttoned and pulled out of the tuxedo pants, his feet bare and his eyes watchful. "I guess I'm not comfortable with unfinished business."

"All right." After lighting a cigar, he leaned back on the railing. "Finish it."

"It isn't as simple as that." A wayward breeze fluttered her hair. She shook it back impatiently. "I was upset and angry before—about there being someone in the house. My house. I know you were concerned and I was very abrupt with you. And after I'd calmed down some I realized you were hurt that I hadn't asked you to help."

He blew out smoke. "I'll get over it."

"It's just that—" She broke off to pace the narrow width of the balcony. No, he wasn't going to make it easier. "I'm used to handling things myself. I've always been the one who's been able to find the logical solution, or the straightest route. It's part of my makeup. When something needs to be done, I do it. I have to, I guess. It's not as though I don't ever want help. It's just . . . it's just that I'm more used to being asked for it, than asking for it myself."

"One of the things I admire about you, Amanda, is the way you get things done." His eyes stayed on hers as he took a long, contemplative drag. "Why don't you tell me what you're going to do about me?"

"I don't know what to do." When her voice rose, she struggled to calm it and started moving again. "I don't like that. I always know what to do if I reason it out long enough. But no matter how much I think it all through, I can't find an answer."

"Maybe that's because two and two don't always make four."

"But they should," she insisted. "They always have for me. All I know is that you make me feel . . . different than I've ever felt before. It scares me." When she whirled back, her eyes were wide and dark with anger. "I know it's easy for you, but not for me."

"Easy for me?" he repeated. "You think this is easy for me?" In two furious motions, he tossed the cigar onto the terrace and ground it out. "I've been on slow burn since the minute I laid eyes on you. That isn't easy on a man, Amanda, believe me."

Because she found it hard to breathe, her voice came out in a whisper. "No one's ever wanted me the way you do. That frightens me." She pressed her lips together. "I've never wanted anyone the way I want you. That terrifies me."

He reached out to snag her hand by the wrist. "Don't expect to say that to me, or look at me the way you look right now, then ask me to let you go."

While panic and excitement warred inside her, she shook her head. "That's not what I'm asking."

"Then spell it out."

"Damn it, Sloan, I don't want you to be reasonable. I don't want to think. I want you to make me stop thinking, right now." On a moan, she threw her arms around him, pressed her lips to his and took exactly what she wanted.

There was fear. She was afraid she was taking a giant step off the edge of a very steep cliff.

There was exhilaration. She was taking that step with her eyes wide open.

And he was with her, all the way. His body was free-falling with hers, caught in the crosswinds, soaring on the current.

"Sloan—"

"Don't say a word." His arms locked tight around her as he pressed his mouth to her throat. The pulse hammering there matched exactly the rhythm of his own. That was what he wanted. That unity. He realized he'd never found it with another woman. "Not a word. Just come inside."

He led her from the balcony to the bedroom, leaving the door open to let in the sunset and the scent of water and flowers. He touched her hair first, watching his own fingers tangle and stroke. Then softly, a whispering touch, his lips on hers. No, he didn't want words from her, because he wasn't certain he could ever find the right ones to tell her what was in his heart. But he could show her.

Unsteady, she braced her hands on his chest. She didn't want to be weak now, but strong. Yet as those lips roamed over her face, she trembled.

Very slowly, barely touching her, he unbuttoned her blouse and slid it from her shoulders. Beneath was a white cotton chemise that made him smile. He should have known that beneath her practical clothes his Amanda would have more practicality. Watching her, he unhooked her slacks so that they slipped to the floor. When she reached out, he took her hands.

"No, just let me touch you. Let me see what it does to you."

Helpless, she closed her eyes as his fingers skimmed, lightly tracing the curve of her breasts. As if she were fashioned of the most delicate glass, he swept those fingertips over her. Elegantly erotic, the fragile caress had the blood rushing under skin, heating it, sensitizing it until she thought she might die from sheer pleasure.

Her head fell back, a shuddering moan escaped as he continued those lazy explorations with patient, gentle hands. He saw the dark delight flicker over her face, felt it shivering through her body. As excitement rioted through him, he circled his thumbs in a whispering touch over the nipples that strained against the cotton. Then his tongue replaced his hands and she gripped frantically at his shoulders for balance.

"Please . . . I can't . . ."

Now she was falling fast and hard, but he was there to catch her. When her knees gave way, he lifted her, cradling her in his arms, covering her mouth with his before laying her on the bed.

"Nobody," she murmured against his lips. "Nobody's ever made love to me like this."

"I'm just getting started."

He was true to his word. With a leisurely pace he took her places she had never been, had her lingering there before gently urging her on. With each touch he opened doors always firmly locked, then left them wide so that light and wind tunneled through. Each time she arched against him, shuddering, he soothed her until she floated down again.

Her taste was enough. Honey here, whiskey there, then as delicate as spun sugar. He filled himself with it, nibbling her skin. Down her arms, her throat, those long, lovely legs. Whenever he was tempted to hurry, to take his own release, he found himself greedy for one more taste.

He skimmed his hands up her ribs, pushing her shirt up, then over her head. At last, at long last, he sampled the smooth skin of her breast. Her hands were in his hair, pressing him closer as colors seemed to shatter behind her eyes.

Slow burn. Is that what he'd said? she wondered frantically as his clever mouth inched lower, still lower. She understood now, now when her body was on fire from the inside, heating degree by degree. The sparks were shooting through her, little pinpoints of un-speakable pleasure as ancient as the first stars that winked to life in the sky beyond the window.

He was tugging the last barrier aside, and she could do nothing but writhe under his hands, the breath sobbing in her lungs.

When he flicked his tongue over her, she arched against him, her hands grabbing at the bedspread in taut fists. Sensations hammered her, too fast, too sharp. She struggled to separate them, but they were one wild maze without beginning or end.

Did she know she was calling out his name over and over? he wondered. Did she know that her body was moving in that slow, sinuous rhythm, as if he were al-ready inside her? He slid up her gradually, savoring each instant, absorbing each ache, each need, each longing. Her eyes fluttered open, dark and dazed.

She could only see his face, so close to hers—his eyes so intense. Gracefully her arms lifted to brush his shirt aside, to touch as thoroughly as she had been touched. She rose to him, to press her lips to his chest, to glide them up to his throat.

The light grew dimmer, softer. The breeze quieted. In an easy dance she moved over him, undressing him, needing to show him what he had done to her heart as well as her body. Her lips curved against his flesh as she felt him tremble as she had trembled. The glory flowed through her like water, clear and bright, so that when her arms came around him, when her mouth opened willingly beneath his, she let it pour into the kiss.

With a murmuring sigh, he slid into her. Her breath caught, then released gently. They moved together, the pace deliberately slow, deliciously easy. The sweetness brought tears to her eyes that he kissed away.

Gradually sweetness became heat, and heat a fresh burning. As passion misted her vision, she felt his fingers link with hers, holding tight as she rode to the top of the crest. His name tumbled from her lips as he swept to the peak with her.

He lay with his lips pressed against her throat, still haunted by the taste of her. Beneath him she was quiet, her breathing deep and steady. He wondered if she slept, and started to ease his weight aside. But her arms slid up and around him again.

"Don't." Her voice was a husky whisper that sent his blood singing again. "I don't want it to end yet."

To satisfy them both, he rolled, reversing positions. Her hair brushed his cheek, a small thing that gave him tremendous happiness. "How's that?"

"Nice." She nuzzled her cheek against his. "It was all really, really nice."

"Is that the best you can do?"

"Umm. For right now. I don't think I've ever been this relaxed in my life."

"Good." Taking her hair in his hand, he pulled her head back to study her face. "It's getting too dark to see." Reaching over, he switched on the light.

Amanda brought up a hand to shield her eyes. "Why'd you do that?"

"Because I want to see you when we make love again."

"Again?" Chuckling, she dropped her head onto his shoulder. "You've got to be kidding."

"No, ma'am. I figure I might just get my fill of you by sunup."

Feeling deliciously lazy, she snuggled against him. "I can't stay the night."

"Wanna bet?"

"No, really." She arched like a cat when he stroked her back. "I wish I could, but I've got a whole list of things to do in the morning. Oh . . ." She shivered under his touch. "You've got such wonderful hands. Wonderful," she murmured as she lost herself in a long, dreamy kiss.

"Stay."

Her body shuddered as she felt him harden inside her. "Maybe for just a little while longer."

Drifting awake, she shifted. On a contented sigh, she reached out. Reluctantly she opened her eyes. Bright sunlight flooded the room, and she was alone in bed. Pushing her tumbled hair back, she sat up.

He'd gotten his way, she thought with a half smile. She had stayed the night, and he hadn't gotten enough of her—or she of him—until sunup.

It had been, she admitted freely, the most magnificent night of her life.

And where the hell was Sloan?

On cue, he walked in, pushing a room service cart. "Morning."

"Good morning." She smiled, though she felt awkward with him dressed and her still naked and in bed.

"I ordered us some breakfast." Sensing her dilemma, he plucked up a white terry-cloth robe from a chair. "Compliments of the BayWatch," he said as he handed it to her, then leaned over a bit farther to give her a leisurely kiss. "Why don't we eat on the terrace?"

"That'd be nice. Give me a minute."

When she joined him outside, there were plates set on the pale azure cloth, and a single rose in a clear vase.

It touched her deeply that he would take as much care with the morning as he had with the night.

"You think of everything."

"Just of you." He grinned as he sat across from her. "We can look at this like a first date, since I never could convince you to have a meal with me before."

"No." Her gaze lowered as she poured coffee for both of them. "I guess you couldn't." Picking up her napkin, she began to pleat it with her fingers. They were having breakfast, she thought, after a long night of feasting. And they'd never even ridden in the same car, shared a pizza, talked on the phone.

It was idiotic, she told herself. It was scary.

"Sloan, I realize this might sound stupid at this stage, but I...I don't make a habit of spending the night with men in hotel rooms. I'm not usually intimate with someone I've known such a short time."

"You don't have to tell me that." He closed a hand over hers until she looked at him. "It's been a fast trip for both of us. Maybe it's because what happened between us is special. I'm in love with you, Amanda. No, don't pull away." He tightened his grip. "Normally I'm a patient man, but I have to work hard on it with you. I'm going to do my best to give you time."

"If I said I was in love with you—" she let out a cleansing breath "—what would happen next?"

In his eyes, something flickered and sent her already unsteady pulse jumping. "Sometimes you can't work out the answers first. You've got to be willing to gamble."

"I've never been much of a gambler." She bit her lip, determined to get over that last skip of fear. "I wouldn't have come here last night if I hadn't been in love with you."

He lifted her hand to press his lips to the palm. Over it, he smiled at her. "I know."

The laugh was as much from relief as amusement. "You knew, but you just had to hear me say it."

"That's right." His eyes were suddenly very sober. "I had to hear you say it. Women aren't the only ones who need words, Amanda."

No, she thought, they weren't. "I love you, but I'm still a little scared of it. I'd like to take it slow, one step at a time."

"Fair enough. We can start by having our first date before the eggs get cold."

At ease, she buttered a piece of toast and split it with him. "You know, as long as I've worked here, I've never sat on one of those terraces and looked out at the bay."

"Never snuck into an empty room and played guest?" He laughed. "No, you wouldn't. You wouldn't even think about it. So, how does it feel, seeing it from the other side of the desk?"

"Well, the bed's comfortable, the hotel robes are roomy and the view's wonderful." There was laughter in her eyes, contented, easy laughter. "However, at The Towers Retreat, we'll offer all that and more. Private spas, romantic fireplaces, complimentary champagne with each reservation—I have to run that by Trent—*cordon bleu* meals prepared by Coco, world-renowned chef, all in a turn-of-the-century setting, complete with ghosts and a legendary hidden treasure." She rested her chin on her hand. "Unless we manage to get our hands on the emeralds before we open."

"Do you really believe they still exist?"

"Yes. Oh, not with any of the mystic business Aunt Coco or Lilah subscribe to. It's simple logic. They did exist. If anyone in the family had sold them, it would have come out. Therefore, they still exist. A quarter of a million in jewels doesn't just disappear.''

His brow lifted. "They're that valuable?"

"Oh, probably more so by now—that's not even counting the aesthetic or intrigue value."

It changed the complexion of things for him entirely. "So what we've got is five women and two kids, who've been living alone in a house loaded with antiques, plus a fortune in jewels. And no security system."

She frowned a little. "It's not exactly loaded with antiques since we've had to sell off a lot over the years. And there's never been a problem. It's not as though any of us are helpless."

"I know. Calhoun women can take care of themselves. I'm beginning to think that besides being tough, they're stupid."

"Now, wait a minute—"

"No, you wait." To emphasize the point, he poked his fork at her. "First thing in the morning, we're going to see about an alarm system."

She'd already decided the same thing herself after yesterday's incident. But that didn't mean he could tell her to. "You're not going to start taking over my life."

"So, to be stubborn, you'll ignore the obvious, because I brought it up, and take a chance that someone might break in and hurt one of the kids."

"Don't put words in my mouth," she tossed back. "I've been checking into alarms for the past two weeks."

"Why didn't you just say so?"

"Because you were too busy handing out orders."
She might have said more, but the horn on one of the
tourist boats distracted her. "What time is it?"

"About one."

"One?" Her eyes went huge. "In the afternoon?
That's not possible, we just got up."

"It's real possible when you don't get to sleep until
morning."

"I've got a million things to do." She was already
pushing back from the table. "All that mess from the
wedding has to be cleaned up. Trent's father was coming for brunch two hours ago, and William's coming by
at three."

"Hold it." That brought him out of his chair.
"You're not still going to see him?"

"Mr. St. James? He'll be gone by now. I can't believe I was so rude."

"William," he corrected, snagging her arm. "The
attractive, intelligent man you had dinner with the
other night."

"William? Well, of course I'm going to see him."

"No." He tugged her closer. "You're not."

The dangerous light in his eyes set off one in her
own. "I just told you you weren't going to take over my
life."

"I don't give a damn what you told me. There's no
way in hell I'm going to let you waltz out of my bed
and on to a date with another man."

With a little huff, she pulled her arm free. "You
don't *let* me do anything. Get that straight. Next, it
isn't a date. William Livingston is an antique dealer
and I promised him I would show him through The
Towers. He gets a busman's holiday, and I get a free
assessment. Now move." She shoved past and headed

for the shower. Muttering all the way, she slipped off the robe. She'd just finished adjusting the water temperature, stepping in and shutting the curtain when it was yanked open again.

"Damn it, Sloan!" She slicked the wet hair out of her eyes and glared.

"He's an antique dealer?"

"That's what I said."

"And he wants to look at furniture?"

"Exactly."

He hooked his thumbs in his belt loops. "I'm going with you."

"Fine." With a careless shrug, she picked up the soap and began to lather her shoulders. "Be a possessive bubblehead."

"Okay."

Telling herself she wasn't amused, she glanced over to see him pulling off his shirt. "What are you doing?"

Grinning, he tossed it aside. "I'll give you three guesses. A sharp lady like you should get it in one."

She bit back a chuckle as he unsnapped his jeans. "I don't have time for water games right now."

"Oh, I think we can sneak it in just under the wire."

"Maybe." She squeezed the wet soap between her hands and shot it at him, nodding approval when he caught it, chest high. "If you wash my back first."

Before stepping from his car, Livingston checked his microrecorder and the tiny camera in his pocket. He was very fond of technology and felt that the sophisticated equipment lent an air of elegance to the job. Since the moment he'd read about the Calhoun emeralds, he'd been obsessed by them, more than any other jewels he'd stolen in his long career. He was considered by Interpol, and indeed by himself, to be one of the most clever and elusive thieves on two continents.

The emeralds presented a challenge he couldn't resist. They weren't tucked in a vault or displayed in a museum. They weren't adoring some rich matron's neck. They were lying in wait somewhere in the odd old house, daring someone to find them. He intended to be that someone.

Though he wasn't opposed to employing violence in his work, he used it sparingly. He was sorry he'd had to use it on Amanda the day before, but he was much sorrier that she'd interrupted his search.

His own fault, he chided himself as he walked to the front door of The Towers. He'd been impatient and had decided that the wedding would be the perfect diversion, giving him the time and the privacy he required to case the interior of the house. Today, however, he would wander those rooms as a guest.

He might have been a thief from the South Side of Chicago, but when he put on a two-thousand-dollar suit, a trace of a British accent and polished manners, even the most discriminating invited him into their parlors.

He knocked and waited. The barking of the dog answered first, and Livingston's eyes hardened. He detested dogs, and the little bugger inside had nearly nipped him before he'd managed to give it a dose of phenobarbital.

When Coco answered the door, Livingston's eyes were clear and his charming smile already in place.

"Mr. Livingston, how nice to see you again." Coco started to offer a hand, then found it more judicious to grasp Fred's collar before the dog could leap at the man's calf. "Fred, stop that now. Mind your manners." Holding the snarling dog at bay, Coco offered a weak smile. "He really is a very gentle animal. He never acts like this, but he had an incident yesterday and isn't himself." After gathering Fred into her arms, she called for Lilah. "Let's go into the parlor, shall we?"

"I hope I'm not intruding on your Sunday, Mrs. McPike. I couldn't resist persuading Amanda to show me through your fascinating house."

"We're delighted to have you." Though she was becoming more disconcerted by the moment as Fred continued to snarl and snap. "Amanda's not here yet, though I can't think what's keeping her. She's always so prompt."

Lilah gave a half laugh as she came down the steps. "I can think exactly what's keeping her." There was no humor in her eyes as she studied their guest. "Hello again, Mr. Livingston."

"Miss Calhoun." He didn't care for the way she looked at him, as though she could see straight through the slick outer trappings to the ruthlessness inside.

"Fred's a bit high-strung today." With a quick pleading look, Coco passed the growling pup to Lilah. "Why don't you take him in the kitchen?" Her hands fluttered before she patted her hair. "Perhaps some herbal tea would soothe him."

"I'll take care of him." Lilah started down the hall, murmuring to the puppy, "I don't like him, either, Fred. Why do you suppose that is?"

"Well then." Relieved, Coco smiled again. "How about some sherry? You can enjoy it while I show you a particularly nice japanned cabinet. It's Charles II, I believe."

"I'd be delighted." He was also delighted to note that she was wearing an excellent set of pearls with matching earrings.

When Amanda arrived twenty minutes later, with Sloan stubbornly at her side, she found her aunt telling Livingston the family history while they admired an eighteenth-century credenza.

"William, I'm so sorry I'm late."

"Don't be." Livingston took one look at Sloan and concluded his entryway to The Towers wouldn't be Amanda after all. "Your aunt has been the most charming and informative of hostesses."

"Aunt Coco knows more about the furnishings than any of us," she told him. "This is Sloan O'Riley. Sloan is the architect who's designing the renovations."

"Mr. O'Riley." The handshake was brief. Sloan had already taken a dislike to the three-piece-suited, sherry-sipping antique dealer. "The work here must present quite a challenge."

"Oh, I'm getting by."

"I was just telling William how slow and tedious the job of sifting through all those old papers is. Not at all the exciting treasure the press makes it out to be." Coco beamed. "But I've decided to hold another séance. Tomorrow night, the first night of the new moon."

Amanda struggled not to groan. "Aunt Coco, I'm sure William isn't interested."

"On the contrary." He turned all his charm on Coco while a plan formed in his mind. "I'd love to attend myself, if I didn't have pressing business."

"The next time then. Perhaps you'd like to go upstairs—"

Before she could finish, Alex burst through the terrace doors, followed by a speeding Jenny and a laughing Suzanna. All three had dirt streaked on their hands and jeans. Eyes narrowed, Alex skidded to a halt in front of Livingston.

"Who's that?" he demanded.

"Alex, don't be a brat." Suzanna snagged his hand before he could spread any of his dirt over the buff-colored tailored pants. "I'm sorry," she began. "We've been in the garden. I made the mistake of mentioning ice cream."

"Don't apologize." Livingston forced his lips to curve. If he disliked anything more than dogs, it was small, grubby children. "They're...lovely."

Suzanna squeezed her son's hand before he could resort to violence at the term. "No, they're not," she said cheerfully. "But we're stuck with them. We'll just get out of your way." As she dragged them off to the kitchen, Alex shot a last look over his shoulder.

"He has mean eyes," he told his mother.

"Don't be silly." She tousled his hair. "He was just annoyed because you almost ran into him."

But Alex looked solemnly at Jenny, who nodded. "Like the snake on Rikki-Tikki-Tavi."

"You move, I strike," Alex said in a fair imitation of the evil cartoon voice.

"Okay, guys, you're giving me the creeps." She laughed off the quick shiver. "The last one in the kitchen has to wash the bowls." She gave them a head start while she rubbed the chill from her arms.

Nine

"There, you see." Amanda gave Sloan a quick kiss on the cheek. "That wasn't so bad."

He wasn't quite ready to be placated. "He hung around for five hours. I don't see why Coco had to invite him for dinner."

"Because he's a charming, and single man." She laughed and slipped her arms around his neck. "Remember the tea leaves."

They stood at the seawall, inside an ornate pergola. Sloan decided it was as good a time as any to nibble on her neck. "What tea leaves?"

"The ones that...mmm. The ones that told Aunt Coco that there would be a man coming along who'd be important to us."

He switched to her ear. "I thought that was me."

"Maybe." She gave a surprised yip when he bit her. "Savage."

"Sometimes the Cherokee in me takes over."

She leaned back to study his face. In the bleeding lights of sunset, his skin was almost copper, his eyes so dark a green they were nearly black. Yes, she could see both sides of his heritage, the Celtic and the Cherokee, both warriors, in those knife-edged cheekbones, the sculpted mouth, the wild reddish hair.

"I really don't know anything about you." Yet it hadn't been like making love to a stranger. When he had touched her, she'd known everything. "Just that you're an architect from Oklahoma who went to Harvard."

"You know I like beer and long-legged women."

"There's that."

Because he could see it was important to her, he sat on the wall, his back to the sea. "Okay, Calhoun, what do you want to know?"

"I don't want to interrogate you." The old nerves resurfaced, making it impossible for her to settle. "It's just that you know everything about me, really. My family, my background, my ambitions."

Because he enjoyed watching her move, he took out a cigar, lighted it, then began to speak. "My great-great-grandfather left Ireland for the New World, and headed west to trap beaver. A genuine mountain man. He married a Cherokee woman, and hung around long enough to get three sons. One day he went off trapping and never came back. The sons started a trading post, did pretty well. One of them sent for a mail-order bride, a nice Irish girl. They had a passel of kids, including my grandfather. He was, and is, a wily old devil who bought up land while it was cheap enough, then hung on until he could sell it at a profit. Keeping up family tradition, he married Irish, a redheaded spitfire who supposedly drove him crazy. He must have loved her a lot, because he named the first oil well after her.''

Amanda, who had been charmed thus far, blinked. ''Oil well?''

''He called it Maggie,'' Sloan said with a grin as he blew out smoke. ''She got such a kick out of it, he gave names to the rest of them, too.''

''The rest of them,'' Amanda said faintly.

''My father took over the company in the sixties, but the old man hasn',t stopped putting his two cents in. He's still ticked that I didn't go into the company, but I wanted to build, and I figured Sun Industries didn't need me.''

''Sun Industries?'' She nearly choked. It was one of the biggest conglomerates in the country. ''You—I had no idea that you had money.''

''My family does, anyway. Problem?''

''No. I just wouldn't want you to think that I…'' She trailed off helplessly.

''That you were after the family fortune?'' He let out a hoot of laughter. ''Honey, I know you were after my body.''

He had the uncanny ability to make her want to swear and laugh at the same time. ''You really are a conceited jerk.''

He tossed the cigar aside before making a grab for her. ''But you love me.''

''Maybe I do.'' With pretended reluctance, she slipped her arms around him. ''A little.'' On a laugh, she lifted her lips to his. His mouth started off teasing, then heated with demands. His hands were light, then impatient, until she was wrapped tight around him, pouring herself mindlessly into the kiss.

"How do you do that to me?" she murmured as he nipped at her moist, parted lips.

"Do what?"

"Make me want you until it hurts."

On an unsteady moan, he pressed his lips to her throat. "Let's go inside. You can show me my room."

She tilted her head to give his busy mouth more freedom. "What room?"

"The room where we'll pretend I'm going to sleep when I'm sleeping with you."

"What are you talking about?"

"I'm talking about making love with you until we both need oxygen." Because he knew he was on the point of dragging her down on the hard, cold tiles, he set her away from him. "And I'm talking about the fact that I'm staying here until the alarm system's operational."

"But you don't need—"

"Oh, I need." He crushed his mouth to hers again to show her how much.

She waited for him, chiding herself for being as nervous as a new bride on her wedding night. Perhaps the waiting was more intense because she knew what they would bring to each other.

She slipped on a thin blue chemise, an impulsive extravagance that had been folded away for months. Unable to settle, she turned down the bed. There were candles she'd kept at the bedside and on the bureau for emergencies. But when she lighted them now, their glow was soft, romantic, and anything but practical. Suzanna had placed flowers in the room, as she always did. This time they were fragile lilies of the valley that added a haunting fragrance. Though there was no moonlight, she opened the terrace doors to let in the steady roar of the water on rocks.

Then he came to her, as she stood in the open doorway with the black night at her back.

The quick joke he'd meant to make melted from his mind. He could only stare, his hand growing damp on the knob, his heart bounding up to block his throat. To have her waiting for him, looking so desirable in the flicker of candlelight, to see that smile of welcome, was everything he'd ever wanted.

He wanted to be gentle with her, as he'd been so carefully gentle the night before. But when he crossed to her, the slow burn had already turned to fire. There was challenge instead of nerves in her eyes as she lifted her arms to take him in.

"I thought you'd never get here," she said, and, led by her own needs, crushed her mouth to his.

How could there be gentleness when there was such heat? How could there be patience when there was such urgency? Her body was already vibrating—Lord, he could feel each wild beat—as it fit itself to his. The flimsy material of her chemise teased the bare flesh of his chest, daring him to rip it aside and plunder. Her scent had wrapped itself around his system, taunting with dark secrets, seducing with fevered promises.

In that moment he was so full of her, he couldn't find himself.

Breathless, disoriented, he lifted his head. He knew his hands were big and could be rough if his heart didn't guide them. He knew his needs were huge and could be ruthless if he didn't retain control.

"Wait." He needed a moment to get back his breath and his sanity, but she was shaking her head.

"No." Her hands clutched in his hair, and she pulled him back to her.

She didn't know when the recklessness had burst through her, but it held sway now, as she fell with him onto the bed. Aggressive and desperate, her hands streaked over him. No weakness this time. No submission. She wanted the power, the power of knowing she could make him careless, make him as mindless and vulnerable as he made her.

In a tangle of arms and legs they rolled over the bed. Each time he tried to pull back, she was there, her mouth greedy, her low, sultry laughter pounding in his blood.

Her busy fingers rushed to unsnap his jeans, then tugged the denim over his hips. His muscles jumped and quivered when she danced those fingertips across his stomach. He swore, snatching her hands before she could drag him over that last jagged edge.

Breath heaving, he stared down at her, her wrists trapped in his hand. Her eyes were like cobalt, glistening dark in the shifting light. He could hear, over his own ragged breaths, the steady ticking of the bedside clock.

Then she smiled, a slow, lazy smile full of knowledge. And he heard nothing but the roar of his own needs.

Hot with hunger, his mouth fused with hers. Reckless with passion, his hands sought and took. She answered, demand for demand, pleasure for pleasure. Control snapped—he could almost hear the chain break as he sated himself with her. This was liberation, a world without reason. Desperate to feel her, he tore the chemise aside. Her quick gasp of surprise only fueled the fires.

Tossed in the whirlwind, she gave herself over to the speed, surrendered herself to the fury. No thought. No question. Only hot, damp flesh, ravenous, searching lips, quick, greedy hands.

His eyes open, fixed on hers, he drove himself into her, letting the shock of pleasure fill them both. Then she was rising up to meet him so that they drove each other into the dark.

"Yes, Mr. Stenerson." Amanda hummed a tune in her head as her supervisor droned on. And on. Ten more minutes, and she was off duty. Even the upcoming séance didn't dim her pleasure.

She would be with Sloan soon. Maybe there would be time for a walk before dinner.

"You don't seem to have your mind on your work, Miss Calhoun."

That brought her back with a jolt of guilt. "You were concerned about Mr. and Mrs. Wicken's complaint."

Glaring, he tapped his pencil on the desk. "I'm very concerned that one of our waiters spilled an entire tray of drinks in Mrs. Wicken's lap."

"Yes, sir. I arranged to have her slacks cleaned, and for a complimentary dinner for them any evening during their stay. They were satisfied."

"And you've fired the waiter?"

"No, sir."

His eyebrows rose up, wiggling like worms. "May I ask why not, when I specifically requested you do so?"

"Because Tim has been with us for three years, and could hardly be blamed for spilling the tray when the little Wicken boy stuck out his foot and tripped him.

Several other waiters, and several of the guests saw it happen.''

"Be that as it may, I gave you a specific order."

"Yes, sir." The cheerful little tune in her head became a throbbing headache. She'd meant to go over all of this with Stenerson before. "And after a closer review of the circumstances, I chose to handle it differently."

"Need I remind you who is in charge of this hotel, Miss Calhoun?"

"No, sir, but I would think after all the years I've worked at the BayWatch, you would trust my judgment." She took a deep breath, and a big risk. "If you don't, it might be best if I turned in my resignation."

He blinked three times, then cleared his throat. "Don't you feel that's a bit rash?"

"No, sir. If you don't feel I'm competent to make certain decisions, it undermines the system."

"It isn't your competence, but your lack of experience. However," he added, holding up a hand, "I'm sure you did what you felt was best in this case."

"Yes, sir."

By the time she left his office, her jaw was clenched. Amanda forced it to relax when William stopped her in the lobby.

"I just wanted to tell you again how much I enjoyed the tour of your home, and the wonderful meal."

"It was our pleasure."

"I have the feeling if I asked you to dinner again, you would have a different reason than hotel policy for saying no."

"William, I—"

"No, no." He patted her hand. "I understand. I'm disappointed, but I understand. I suppose Mr. O'Riley will attend the séance tonight?"

She laughed. "Whether he wants to or not."

"I really am sorry I'll miss it." He gave her hand a final squeeze. "It's at eight, did you say?"

"No, nine, sharp. Aunt Coco will have us all gathered around the dining table holding hands and sending out alpha waves or whatever."

"I hope you'll let me know if you receive any messages from . . . the other side."

"It's a deal. Good night."

"Good night." He glanced at his watch as she left. He had more than enough time to get ready.

"I thought I'd find you here." Amanda stepped into the large circular room the family called Bianca's tower. Lilah was curled on the window seat, as she often was, looking out to the cliffs.

"Yeah, just me and fierce Fred." Coming out of a private dream, she ruffled the dozing dog's fur. "We're getting in tune for tonight's séance."

"Spare me." Amanda plopped onto the seat beside her.

"Well, what's wiped off that satisfied smile you had on your face this morning? Did you fight with Sloan?"

"No."

"Then it must be the dastardly Stenerson." At Amanda's brief oath, Lilah grinned. "Right the second time. Why do you put up with him, Mandy? The man's a weasel."

"Because I work for him."

"So quit."

"Easy for you to say." She shot Lilah an impatient look. "We can't all drift around from day to day like dreamy forest sprites." She cut herself off, letting out a disgusted breath. "Sorry."

Lilah only shrugged. "It sounds like you've got more needling you than Stenerson."

"He started it. He said I didn't have my mind on my work, and he was right."

"So your mind was wandering. Big deal."

"It is a big deal. Damn it, I like my job, and I'm good at it. But I haven't been concentrating, not on that or the necklace, or anything, since..."

"Since the big gun swaggered in from the West."

"It's not funny."

"Sure it is." Lilah wrapped her arms around her knees and rested her chin on them. "So you lose a little concentration, misplace one of your lists or miss an appointment by five minutes. So what?"

"I'll tell you so what. He's changing me and I don't know what to do about it. I have responsibilities, obligations. Damn it, I have goals. I have to think about tomorrow, and five years from tomorrow." The trouble was, when she did, she thought of Sloan. "What if he's just a glitch? A wonderful, exciting glitch that throws off everything I've planned out? A few weeks from now, he finishes up here and heads back to Oklahoma, and my life's a mess."

"What if he asks you to go with him?"

"That's worse." Flustered, Amanda rose to wander in distracted circles. "What am I supposed to do? Throw away everything I've worked for, everything I've hoped for just because he says saddle up?"

"Would you?"

Amanda shut her eyes. "I'm afraid I would."

"Then why don't you talk to him?"

"I can't." She sat again. "We haven't talked about the future. I guess neither of us wants to think about it. It was just that today, I started thinking—"

"You would get back to it."

"I started thinking," Amanda repeated, "that a month ago I didn't even know him. It's crazy to start planning my life around someone I've only known such a short time."

"And you've always been the sensible one," Lilah put in.

"Well, yes."

"Then relax." For encouragement she patted Amanda's shoulder. "When the time comes, you're bound to do the sensible thing."

"I hope you're right," Amanda murmured, then forced herself to add a decisive nod. "Of course, you're right. I'm going to work in the storeroom until dinner."

"See you're back on track already." Lilah chuckled to herself when Amanda strode out. "Come on, Fred." She nuzzled his nose. "Let's go see if we can derail her."

Sloan walked into the storeroom, armed with a bottle of champagne, a wicker basket and some of Lilah's sisterly advice. *Keep her off balance, big guy. The one thing you can't let her do is get logical on you.*

Though he wasn't exactly sure what had prompted Lilah's visit, he approved the spirit of it. Just as he approved the way Amanda looked, hunched over a desk in the storeroom, glasses on her nose, hair clipped back. There were neatly labeled file boxes stacked behind her, dozens of dusty cardboard boxes scattered alongside her and several fat piles of paper in front of her.

"Hey, Calhoun, ready for a break?"

"What?" Her head came up quickly, but it took a moment for her eyes to focus. "Oh, hi. I didn't hear you come in."

"Where were you?"

She lifted a ledger. "Back in 1929. It seems my illustrious great-grandpapa made a little pin money running liquor in from Canada during Prohibition."

"Good old Fergus."

"Greedy old Fergus," she corrected. "But a businessman through and through. If he kept such meticulous books of his illegal activities, he certainly would have a record of sale if he sold the emeralds."

"I thought Bianca hid them."

"That's the legend." She leaned back to rub her tired eyes. "I'd rather have the facts. I had this thought that maybe he put them in a safe-deposit box he didn't tell anyone about. But I can't find any record of that, either."

"Maybe you're looking in the wrong place." He set the bottle and basket down as he stood behind her. Gently he began to massage her neck muscles. "Maybe you should concentrate on Bianca. It was her necklace after all."

"We don't have a lot of information about Bianca." When her eyes started to drift closed, she popped them open again. "Great-Grandpapa destroyed all of her pictures, her letters, just about everything concerning her. We've only come across one of her date books so far."

"He must have been crazy mad."

"Crazy, anyway. Grieving, I'd think."

"No." Bending, he kissed the top of her head. "If he'd been grieving, he would have kept everything."

"Maybe it hurt to remember."

"If he'd loved her, he would have wanted to remember. He would have needed to. When you love someone, everything about them's precious." He felt her muscles knot under his fingers. "What's the problem, Amanda? You're all tied up."

"I've been sitting too long, that's all."

"Then my timing's perfect." He stepped back to pick up the champagne."

"What's that for?"

"Most people drink it." Sloan released the cork. After the pop came the seductive hiss. "I don't know about you, but I worked my butt off today. I thought we'd take a first-class coffee break."

She didn't need champagne to cloud her brain. He did that all by himself. And that, she reminded herself as she rose, was exactly what she needed to avoid. "It's a nice thought, but I should go help Aunt Coco with dinner."

"Lilah's helping her."

"Lilah?" Amanda's brows shot up. "You've got to be kidding."

"Nope." He opened the basket to take out two fluted glasses. "Suzanna's doing homework with the kids, and you and I are having dinner alone."

"Sloan, I'm really not dressed to go out."

"I like you in sweats." He poured the wine and, setting the bottle aside, lifted both glasses. "And we're not going anywhere."

"You just said—"

"I said we were having dinner alone, and we are. Right here."

"Here?" She gestured. "In the storeroom?"

"Yep. I got some of your aunt's pâté, some cold chicken and asparagus, and fresh strawberries." He tapped his glass against hers before drinking. "I've been thinking about you all day."

He didn't even have to try to make her knees weak. When he did sweet things, said sweet things, she dissolved into a puddle of love. "Sloan, we have to talk."

"Sure." But he bent down to rub his lips lazily over hers. "Why don't we get comfortable first?"

"What?" Already dizzy, she stared at him as he took out a blanket and spread it over the floor.

"Come on."

"I really think it would be better if we..." But he was already pulling her down to the blanket.

He took the glass from her hand, setting it on the floor before nuzzling her mouth. "This is better," he murmured. "Much better."

"The children are home," she managed as his hands slid under her shirt. "If someone came in—"

"I locked the door." Gently he skimmed the rough pad of his thumb over her nipples. "Pay attention, Calhoun, I'm going to show you how to relax."

She was so relaxed, she didn't think she could move. Heavy, her eyes fluttered partway open when Sloan lay a smidgen of pâté on her tongue.

"It's good," he told her, then spread a dab on her bare shoulder so he could lick it off. "Here." He lifted her, cradling her against his chest before he handed her the glass of champagne. "We were supposed to drink this first, but I got distracted."

It tasted like sin on her tongue. She sipped again, then opened her mouth obediently when he fed her more pâté, this time on a conventional cracker.

"More?"

She sighed her assent. They began to feed each other tidbits from the basket between kisses. Replete, she watched him pour the last of the champagne. "We're going to be late for the séance."

"Nope." He drew her back more comfortably against his chest. "Coco decided that the vibes weren't right. Something about interference from a dark presence."

"Sounds just like my levelheaded aunt."

"Now she wants to wait until the last night of the new moon." He nuzzled her neck. "We can stay in here all night."

She was beginning to believe that with him, anything was possible. "That would make it my first all-night picnic."

"After we're married, we'll make it a regular event."

Champagne slopped over her hand and onto his leg as she jolted straight.

"Easy, Calhoun, don't waste it."

She struggled around to face him. "What do you mean, married?"

"You know, like man and wife, that kind of thing."

With deliberate care, she set the glass down. Just like that, she thought, both panicked and angry. Just as she'd expected. With him it was *saddle up, Calhoun. We're getting hitched.* "What gave you the idea that we were getting married?"

He didn't like the fact that the line was back between her brows. "I love you, you love me. You're the logical one, Amanda. The next step's marriage from my point of view."

"It may be a step from your point of view, but it's a big leap from mine. You can't just assume I'm going to take it."

"Why not?"

"Because you can't. In the first place, I'm not planning on marriage for years yet. I've got my career to think about."

"What's one got to do with the other?"

"Everything. You've already messed up my concentration, had me shuffling around my priorities." Knowing it sounded foolish, she stopped to drag a hand through her hair. "Look at me," she demanded. "Just look at me. I'm sitting on the storeroom floor, naked, and arguing with a man I've only known for two weeks. This isn't me."

With deceptive laziness, he skimmed his gaze down, then up again. "Then who the hell is it?"

"I don't know." Frantic, she snatched up her sweats and began to pull them on. "I don't know who I am anymore, and it's your fault. Nothing's made sense since you ran into me on the sidewalk."

"You ran into me."

"That's beside the point." Shaken to the core, she yanked the sweatshirt over her head. "I'm daydreaming when I'm supposed to be working. I'm making love with you when I should be keeping appointments. I'm having naked picnics when I should be filing papers. It's got to stop."

"Maybe I should've just hit you over the head with the bottle of champagne instead of letting you drink it." Baffled, he scratched his head. "Why don't you sit down, Calhoun, and we'll talk this thing out?"

"No, I will not sit down. You'll start on me again, and I won't be able to think. You're not going to make plans for the rest of my life without consulting me, without even having the courtesy to ask. I'm taking back control of my life."

He rose then, naked and furious. "You're mad because I want you to marry me."

The breath hissed out between her clenched teeth. "You're just stupid." She grabbed the cl sest thing handy and ended up hurling her glasses at him. "Too stupid for words." With this she strode to the door, fought with and cursed the lock until she managed to open it. "You can take your incredibly romantic proposal and stuff it."

The hot and hazy afternoon was perfect for pleasure. Christian surprised me with a little basket of wine and cold ham. Together we sat in the wild grass beyond the rock and watched the boats glide by below. The light was so golden, like something poured out of a gilded pitcher. But it is always so when I'm with him. In this lovely fantasy of afternoons, there is nothing but sunlight and warm, fragrant air.

We talked of everything and nothing as he sketched me. He has already done two paintings of me since the summer began. Without risking modesty I can say he made me look beautiful. What woman is not when she is in love? And it was his eyes that studied me, his hands that drew my face, my hair. His feelings that guided his brush.

If I had not believed before how deep and true his love is for me, I would have seen it in the portraits he painted.

Will someone buy my portrait from him? It saddens me to think of it. Yet it makes me proud. That would be one way I could at last declare my feelings. Hanging on some pretty wall, the portrait of a woman whose eyes are filled with love for the man who painted her.

I say we talked of everything and nothing. We do not mention how quickly the days fly into weeks. There are so little of those weeks left before I must leave the island, and Christian. I think something in me will die this time.

Fergus and I attended a dinner dance tonight. He was very jolly, though there was much talk of war. He said that clever men know that there will always be war, and money to be made from it. I was stunned to hear him speak so, but he only brushed aside my concern.

"It's for you to think of how to spend the money, and for me to make it," he told me.

It upset me because it was not for money I married him, nor is it for money I stay with him. Both were for duty. Yet I have lived under his roof, eaten his food, taken his gifts without a thought.

It scrapes at my conscience to know that I appreciated the little picnic Christian brought to me so much more than I have ever appreciated all the sumptuous dinners Fergus's money has paid for.

Because it always pleases him, I wore the emeralds, and I have not yet put them away. They lie in the shadowed light, glinting at me, reminding me of both my grief and my joy.

If it were not for the children... but I can't think of it. There are the children. Whatever sins I commit, I will never desert them. They have needs that neither Christian nor I have a right to ignore. I know, in the loneliness ahead of me, they will be solace. Being blessed with them, it is not right to grieve for the child Christian and I must never conceive.

Yet, I do.

Tonight when I turn off the lamp I'll try to sleep quickly. For then it will be morning, and morning will become the golden afternoon, when I can see Christian again.

Ten

The only thing that prevented Amanda from slamming the door was the fact that Suzanna would have already put the children to bed. But she did kick it.

Limping and muttering and occasionally sending a furious look over her shoulder, she started down the hallway. At that point, she wasn't certain if she was more angry with Sloan for taking her assent for granted, or with herself for wanting to give it to him. Marriage hadn't been in her plans, but damn it, she was good at taking the unexpected and making it work. But if he thought she would give him the satisfaction of just hopping on board because he said so, then he didn't know Amanda Kelly Calhoun.

When we get married, she fumed. Not if, not will you or would you. And the problem, the big problem was that under the instant panic and anger had been a thrill. She paused outside of her bedroom door as her own soft sigh caught up with her. Oh, Lord, she did want to marry him. Despite all the good, solid, sensible reasons against it, marrying him was exactly what she wanted. Living with him would mean living with the constant threat of upheaval. She smiled to herself. And what more satisfying life could there be for a woman so skilled at putting things back in place?

With her hand on the doorknob, she hesitated, debating whether she would go back, give in to the urge to throw herself laughing into his arms and say...yes!

No. Resolute, Amanda pushed open the door. She wasn't about to make it that easy for him. If he wanted her, really wanted her, then he was going to have to work a little harder. When he got it right—if he got it right—she corrected as she shut the door behind her, she would smile, slide her arms around him and say—

An arm whipped around her throat and cut off her breath. Instinctively she struggled, throwing both hands up to the barrier to yank and scratch as she fought to drag in the air to scream. Until the hard, cold barrel of a gun pressed against her temple.

"Don't." The voice was only a harsh whisper at her ear. "Be very still, and very quiet, and I won't have to hurt you."

Obediently she let her arms fall limply to her sides, but her mind was speeding. The children were just down the hall. Their safety came first. And Sloan... Sloan could come along at any moment, furiously demanding a showdown.

"That's better." The pressure on her windpipe eased slightly. "If you scream, people are going to get hurt—starting with you. I don't think you want that." She shook her head. "Good. Now—" He swore and tightened his grip again as Sloan bellowed in the corridor.

"Calhoun. I'm not finished with you."

"Be absolutely quiet," the man warned as he dragged her back. "Or I'll kill him."

Amanda shut her eyes and prayed.

Sloan shoved open the door of her room, but it was pitch-dark and silent inside. While he stood in the doorway, swearing, Amanda was pressed back into the corner, knowing the gun was now aimed in Sloan's direction. Her stomach seemed to be packed with ice as she stood, not even daring to breathe, willing him to turn and go. And when he did, when she heard his boots clanging on the stairs, she wondered if she would ever see him again.

"Now that we have a little privacy, we can talk." But the arm stayed around her throat and the gun at her temple. "About the emeralds."

"I don't know where they are."

"Yes. Initially I had trouble believing that, but now I'm sure you don't. So we'll play this a different way. We'll have to move quickly. First the storeroom. I'll take the papers you've yet to sort through. Then, to add a little flare to the trip, we'll fetch Coco's pearls, and a few of the smaller, more portable items."

"You'll never get out of the house."

"You just leave that up to me." There was a faint lilt of pleasure in the voice now, as if he would enjoy the challenge. "Now we're going to move quietly, and very quickly to the storeroom. If you try anything heroic, I'll regret shooting you."

She didn't dare, not with the children so close. But the storeroom, she thought, as she started out with him directly behind her. That was a different matter.

Sloan had left the lights on. The remnants of their picnic were spread over the floor. The air smelled, ever so lightly, of strawberries and champagne.

"Very sweet," Livingston murmured, then shut the door behind them. "It would have been more convenient for me if you had had the séance instead of a tryst." He loosened his hold so that she could step away, but kept his gun level.

Amanda stared at the man she knew as William Livingston. He was all in black with a soft leather pouch worn crosswise over his chest. On his hands were thin surgical gloves. The gun he carried was small, but she didn't doubt it was lethal, not when she looked into his eyes.

"No recriminations, Amanda?" His brow lifted when she said nothing. "I'd hoped you and I could enjoy each other while I was conducting business, but . . . let's not waste time." From his pouch he pulled out a denim duffel bag. "Just the papers from those boxes there. I'm sure you're too efficient to have filed away anything useful."

She bent to pick up the bag he'd tossed at her. "You've lost your accent."

"It's lost its purpose. Be quick, Amanda." His eyes narrowed as he gestured with the gun. "Very quick."

She began to stuff papers into the bag. He was stealing her history, she thought furiously. Her family. "These won't do you any good."

"I doubt you believe that, or you wouldn't be wasting your time with them." His posture seemed almost relaxed now as he stood between Amanda and the door. "You're much too practical. In my profession, it pays to do your homework. I know your family quite well." To hurry her along, he waved the gun. "Which is why I chose to concentrate on you, the most efficient and straightforward of the Calhoun women."

If his ego was the only thing she could strike at, she'd take her best shot. "I hope you weren't expecting me to fall for you." She flicked a coolly dismissive glance over him. "You're not my type—then or now."

It hit the mark. His vanity was as huge as his ambition. "It's a pity that the lack of time prevents me from testing that. Perhaps when I come back, we'll pick up where we left off."

"Even if you get away tonight, you'll never get back in this house again."

He only smiled. "We'll see. Running into you like this complicates my plans, but it doesn't alter the final goal. The necklace. I want it very badly. Some jewels have power, and I have a feeling about this necklace. A strong feeling."

The air in the room was suddenly cold, bone-chilling cold. The expression in Livingston's eyes changed. "Drafts," he muttered uneasily. "The place is full of drafts."

But Amanda felt it, too, and was Calhoun enough to recognize it.

"It's Bianca," she said, and despite the gun, despite the odds, felt completely safe. "If you've done your homework, then you'll know she's still here." The darting nerves in his eyes made her smile. "I don't think she wants you to have the papers, or the necklace."

"Ghosts?" he laughed, but the sound was strained. Though he could see with his own eyes that nothing had changed, he was no longer sure he was alone in the room with Amanda. "That's unworthy of you."

"Then why are you frightened?"

"I'm not frightened, I'm in a hurry. That's enough." He found himself desperate to get out of the room, out of the house. Despite the eerie chill, a line of sweat dribbled down his back. "You carry the bag. Since this has taken longer than expected, we'll have to forgo Coco's pearls, for now." Impatient, he waved the gun at her. "Out the terrace doors."

Amanda debated heaving the duffel bag at him and running. But then he would have the papers. Instead, she struggled with it, then fumbled at the door. "It's stuck."

She was braced when he came up behind her to fight with the old latch. The minute the door opened, she stuck a foot behind him, threw her weight against him, then ran.

Wanting to lead him away from her family, she headed toward the west wing. As she hit the first set of stone stairs, she shouted for Sloan. The heavy bag bumped each step as she dragged it with her. She could hear him behind her, closing in, and zigged around a corner as the first bullet pinged off granite.

She didn't stop to catch her breath, though her lungs were beginning to burn. The May night was warm, oppressively warm after the cold of the storeroom. The air was heavy with the threat of rain.

The sensation of safety she had felt in the storeroom had vanished. There was no protection now, except for her knowledge of the complex layout of the terraces and stairs. But she was straining, fighting her way through the dark and through the sudden certainty that she could not handle this alone.

Then she saw Sloan, heading toward her from the opposite direction. The relief lasted only an instant before she heard another shot.

Lights were flashing everywhere inside the house. Sloan shouted at her before he came forward like a charging bull. Unarmed, Amanda realized, blind with fury, and straight into a loaded gun.

Without hesitation, she whirled away from Sloan and heaved the bag of papers at Livingston. As he snatched it up, she could hear raised voices from inside, Jenny's crying, the dog's frantic barks. Wanting to protect as much as be protected, Amanda raced toward Sloan. When she reached him, arms outstretched, he shoved her aside.

"Get in the house."

"He's got a gun," she said, desperately clinging to his arm. "Just let him go."

"I said get inside." He shook her off, then before her astonished eyes, leaped over the wall.

With her heart in her throat, she raced to it, to see him scrambling up from the terrace below. Even as Lilah burst through a door, Amanda was giving chase.

"What the hell's going on?" Lilah shouted after her.

"Call the police." After the single order, Amanda saved her breath for running, following the sound of stampeding feet and Fred's furious barks.

There was no moonlight to guide her, but she plunged heedlessly into the dark, screaming for Sloan when she heard the explosion of gunfire. She flew down the steps, tearing around the house in a dead run. Over her own ragged gasps, she heard a shouted curse, then the sound of tires squealing on asphalt.

In her hurry, she stumbled once, scrambling back up from the driveway with gravel stinging her palms. Then for an instant, a terrifying instant, there was only the sound of the sea and the wind and her own thundering pulse.

Her legs trembled as she dashed down the slope, so blind with fear that she didn't see Sloan until she rammed into him.

"Oh, God." Her hands were instantly on his face. "I thought he'd killed you."

He was too infuriated at having lost his quarry to appreciate her concern. "Not for lack of trying. Are you all right?"

"Yes, yes, I'm fine. It was—"

"You're bleeding." Every other thought in his head vanished. "There's blood on your hands."

"I fell." She dropped her head onto his shoulder. "It was so dark, and I couldn't see." Fighting tears, she held on to him as Fred whined at their feet. In an abrupt change of mood, she pulled back, pushing at his chest with her sore hands. Her damp eyes sizzled. "Are you crazy, chasing after him that way? I told you he had a gun. He could have shot you."

"He damn near shot you," Sloan retorted. "And didn't I tell you to stay inside?"

"I don't take orders from you," she began.

"You're both alive," Lilah commented. Flashlight in hand, she strolled toward them. "I could hear you arguing from the end of the driveway." The light shot across papers scattered in the road. "What's all this?"

"Oh, God, he must have dropped some." Amanda was already down on her hands and knees, gathering them up.

"Must've been when Fred bit his leg." Far from pacified, Sloan bent to snatch up a paper before it blew away.

"Fred bit him?" Amanda and Lilah said in unison.

"Good and hard from the sound of it." It was a small but sweet satisfaction. "We might have had him, too, but he had a car stashed down the road."

"And he might have shot both of you," Amanda retorted.

"Excuse me." Lilah felt she was doing her part by shining the light so they could see to find papers. "Who is he?"

"Livingston," Sloan told her, then added a string of curses. "You'll have to get the details from your sister."

"Inside," Lilah suggested. "The rest of the family is in an uproar."

"You called the police?"

"Yes." Right before she'd rushed out of the house, barefoot, to chase her sister down the graveled driveway. When Fred stopped to perk his ears then give a long, ululant howl, she laughed. "And I'd say they're on the way. Fred already hears the sirens."

Because her arms were full, Amanda pushed the papers into Lilah's arms, then began to pick up more as they started back. "He didn't get everything," she muttered, then thought of that moment in the storeroom when the air had changed. "I knew he wouldn't."

At the door of the house Suzanna stood, a slim gladiator, armed with a fireplace poker. "Is everyone all right?"

"Fine." Amanda let out an exhausted breath. "The kids?"

"In the parlor with Aunt Coco. Oh, honey, your hands."

"I just scraped them."

"I'll get some antiseptic."

"And some brandy," Lilah added, before laying the papers on a table in the hallway.

Twenty minutes later, the story had been related to the police, and the family was left alone to absorb it. Sloan paced behind the sofa while the Calhoun women huddled together.

"We had that—that thief to dinner." Coco glared into her brandy. "I baked a chocolate soufflé. And all the time he was plotting to steal from us."

"The police will shoot him," Alex piped up. "Bang! Between the eyes."

"I think we've had enough excitement for one night." Suzanna kissed the top of his head. Less sure of himself than he wanted to be, Alex slipped a hand into hers and held tight.

"He got most of the papers." With a sigh, Amanda reached for the pile she'd tossed onto the coffee table. "I hope Fred took a good chunk out of him."

"Good boy, Fred." Lilah cuddled the dog in her lap. "I don't think they'll do Livingston—or whoever he is—any good. He's not meant to find the emeralds. We are."

"He won't get the chance," Sloan said grimly. "Not with the security system I'm putting in." He shot a look at Amanda, daring her to argue, but she was staring at one of the papers.

"It's a letter," she murmured. "A letter from Bianca to Christian."

"Oh, my dear." Coco leaned forward. "What does it say?"

Amanda read,

"My love,
I'm writing this as the rain continues to fall and

keeps me from you. I wonder what you are doing, if you paint today in the gloomy light and think of me. When I'm alone like this in my tower, separated from the reality of my duties, I let the memories sweep over me. Of the first time I saw you, standing on the cliffs. Of the last time I touched you. I'm praying for the sun, Christian, so that we can make more memories. I cannot tell you how you have changed me, how much more my eyes see, now that they see with my heart. I can't imagine how empty my life would have been without this time we had together. I know now that love is very rare, very precious. It is something to be cherished and held on to tightly while too often it is smothered, or brushed carelessly away. Remember, even when our time together ends, I will hold your love. It will live in my heart long after that heart stops beating.

Bianca."

Coco let out a long, dreamy sigh. "Oh, how much they must have loved each other."

"Yucky," Alex said sleepily, and rested his head on his mother's breast.

Amanda smoothed the letter out, hating the fact that it had become crumpled. "I guess she never got the chance to send it to him. All these years it's been mixed up with receipts and account sheets."

"And tonight *we* found it, not Livingston," Lilah reminded her.

"Luck," Amanda murmured.

"Fate," her sister insisted.

When the phone rang, Amanda was the first up to answer. "It's the police," she said, then settled back to listen. "I see. Yes, thank you for letting us know." She hung up, blowing out a disgusted breath. "Looks like he got away. He didn't go back to the BayWatch for any of his things, or he slipped in and took what he wanted and left the rest."

"Do they think he'll come back?" Alarmed, Coco patted her chest.

"No, but they're going to keep an eye on the house until they're sure he's left the island."

"I imagine he's halfway to New York by now." Suzanna shifted the drowsy children on her lap. "And if he comes back, we'll be ready for him."

"More than ready," Amanda agreed. "They have an APB out, but . . . I guess that's all that can be done for tonight."

"No." Sloan crossed the room to her. "There's a little more that has to be done." He nodded to the rest of the room as he pulled her toward the doorway. "You'll excuse us."

"They might, but I don't," Amanda told him. "Let go of my arm."

"Okay." He did, then nipping her by the waist, hauled her over his shoulder. "It's always the hard way with you."

"I will not be slung around like a sack of potatoes." As he climbed the stairs, she wriggled, trying for one clear shot with her foot.

"We left some loose ends before you stormed off to go tangle with an armed robber. Now we're damn well going to tie them up. You like straight talk, Calhoun, and you're about to get some."

"You don't know what I like." She slammed a fist into his back. "You don't know anything."

"Then it's time I found out." He kicked open the door of her room, stalked over and dumped her onto the bed. When she scrambled up, fists raised, he shoved her down again. "You sit where I put you. So help me, we're going to have this out once and for all."

Amanda stunned them both by covering her face with her hands and bursting into tears. She couldn't stop them. Everything that had happened in the past few hours reared up to set off an emotional jag that knocked her flat. On an oath, Sloan stepped toward her, then away, then dragged a helpless hand through his hair.

"Don't do that, Mandy."

She only shook her head and continued to sob.

"Come on now, please." His voice gentled as he crouched in front of her. "I didn't mean to make you cry." Lost, he stroked her hair, patted her shoulder. "I'm sorry, honey. I know you've been through hell tonight. I should have waited to start on this." Cursing himself, he rubbed her arm. "Look, you can hit me if it'd make you feel better."

She sniffled, drew in a hitching breath, then clipped him hard enough to send him sprawling. Through a veil of tears, she studied him as he dabbed at his mouth with the back of his hand.

"I forgot how literal minded you were." He sat where he was as they watched each other. "You finished crying?"

"I think so." Sniffling again, she dug into her pocket for a tissue. "Your lip's bleeding."

"Yeah." He started to reach for the tissue, but she was wiping her face with it. Laughing, he sat back again. "God Almighty, you're a piece of work."

"I'm glad you think this whole thing is a big joke. Men breaking into the house, waving guns around. You're lucky I didn't find you facedown in the road with a hole in your head."

He saw the tears welling again and took her hands. "Is that what this is about?" He pressed a kiss to her freshly bandaged palms. "You're upset because I went after him?"

"I told you not to."

"Hey." His gaze fixed on hers, he raised a hand to cup her chin. "Do you think I could stand around after he'd taken a potshot at you? The only thing I regret is that I didn't catch up with him, so I could rearrange that pretty face of his."

"That's just stupid machismo," she said, but turned her cheek into his hand.

"That's the second time tonight you've called me stupid. I'd like to get back to the first time."

Instantly she pulled back and pokered up. "I don't want to talk about it."

"Too bad. That little chase was quite a diversion, but it's done now. We're not. How come you jumped all over me when I mentioned marriage?"

"Mentioned it? You ordered it."

"I just said that—"

"You just assumed," she interrupted, then pushed by him to stand up. "Just because I love you, just because I've made love with you, doesn't give you any right to take me for granted. I told you before that I make my own plans."

"I've had it with your plans, Calhoun." He took her arm to hold her still. "I've got plans, too, and needs. It so happens they all include you. I love you, damn it." He emphasized the point with a quick, frustrated shake. "You're the only woman I've ever needed, really needed. The only woman I've ever wanted to spend my life with, have children with, make a home with. God knows why when you're as ornery as a mule with two heads, but that's the way it is."

"Then why didn't you just ask?"

Baffled, he shook his head. "Ask what?"

She made a strangled sound and began to pace again. "It's not like I'm asking for Byron or Shelley. I don't expect you to get down on your knees with a hand over your heart. Maybe a little violin music wouldn't have hurt," she muttered. "Or some candlelight."

"Violin music?"

"Forget it." She stopped, hands on her hips, to face him down. "Do you think just because I'm sensible and organized that I don't need any trappings, any romance? You come here, change my entire life, make me love you so much I can't see straight, then you don't even have the good sense to do it right."

"Hold on." He held up a hand before she could stride by him again. "Are you saying you're mad because I didn't ask you fancy enough?"

The sound came again, louder this time. Her face was flushed with temper, her eyes glowing with it. "You didn't ask at all, but why should you? You already know the answer."

Trying to figure women, he thought while he rubbed his hands over his face, was like... trying to figure women. "You wait here," he told her, and strode out.

"Typical," Amanda called after him, then plopped down onto the bed. She was still stewing, her chin on her hand, when he came back in. "Now what?" she demanded.

"Just shut up a minute." He set the tape recorder he'd borrowed on her dresser, then pulled out a pack of matches. Systematically he began to light candles, moving from one part of the room to another while she scowled at him. When he was satisfied, he turned off the lights.

"What are you doing?"

"I'm getting things ready so I can ask you to marry me without having you throw something at me again."

Chin up, she jumped out of bed. "Now you're making fun of me."

"No, I'm not. Damn it, woman, are you going to argue with me all night or let me try to do this right?"

There was enough exasperation in his voice to make her stop and consider him. He didn't look terribly comfortable, she noted. And because he didn't, she wanted to smile. He was doing it for her, she realized. Because he loved her.

"I guess I'll let you try. What's that?" he asked, gesturing to the tape recorder.

"It's Lilah's." He punched the Play button. The soft, weeping sound of violins flowed into the room. Now she did smile, though her heart was beginning to thud.

"It's lovely."

"So are you, I should have made a point of telling you that more often." Stepping toward her, he held out a hand.

"Now's a good time to start." She placed her hand in his.

"I love you, Amanda." Very gently, he touched his lips to hers. "I love everything about you. The woman who makes lists and lines up her shoes in the closet. The woman who goes swimming in freezing water, just so she can be alone for a while. I love the incredibly sexy woman I found in bed, and the tough one, who knows her own mind. It's all the things you are I don't want to live without.''

"I love you, too.'' She lifted a hand to his face. "I meant it when I said you'd changed my life. Tonight, when I read Bianca's letter, I understood how she felt. I'll never feel about anyone the way I feel about you. I'll never want to.''

Smiling, he caught her wrist, turning it so that he could brush a kiss over her hand. "Then you're going to marry me?''

She laughed as she threw her arms around him. "I thought you'd never ask.''

* * * * *

MILLION DOLLAR JACKPOT
SWEEPSTAKES RULES & REGULATIONS
NO PURCHASE NECESSARY TO ENTER OR RECEIVE A PRIZE

1. Alternate means of entry: Print your name and address on a 3″ ×5″ piece of plain paper and send to the appropriate address below.

In the U.S.	In Canada
MILLION DOLLAR JACKPOT	MILLION DOLLAR JACKPOT
P.O. Box 1867	P.O. Box 609
3010 Walden Avenue	Fort Erie, Ontario
Buffalo, NY 14269-1867	L2A 5X3

2. To enter the Sweepstakes and join the Reader Service, affix the Four Free Books and Free Gifts sticker along with both of your other Sweepstakes stickers to the Sweepstakes Entry Form. If you do not wish to take advantage of our Reader Service, but wish to enter the Sweepstakes only, do not affix the Four Free Books and Free Gifts sticker; affix only the Sweepstakes stickers to the Sweepstakes Entry Form. Incomplete and/or inaccurate entries are ineligible for that section or sections of prizes. Torstar Corp. and its affiliates are not responsible for mutilated or unreadable entries or inadvertent printing errors. Mechanically reproduced entries are null and void.

3. Whether you take advantage of this offer or not, on or about April 30, 1992, at the offices of D.L. Blair, Inc., Blair, NE, your sweepstakes numbers will be compared against the list of winning numbers generated at random by the computer. However, prizes will only be awarded to individuals who have entered the Sweepstakes. In the event that all prizes are not claimed, a random drawing will be held from all qualified entries received from March 30, 1990 to March 31, 1992, to award all unclaimed prizes. All cash prizes (Grand to Sixth) will be mailed to winners and are payable by check in U.S. funds. Seventh prize will be shipped to winners via third-class mail. These prizes are in addition to any free, surprise or mystery gifts that might be offered. Versions of this Sweepstakes with different prizes of approximate equal value may appear at retail outlets or in other mailings by Torstar Corp. and its affiliates.

4. PRIZES: (1) *Grand Prize $1,000,000.00 Annuity; (1) First Prize $25,000.00; (1) Second Prize $10,000.00; (5) Third Prize $5,000.00; (10) Fourth Prize $1,000.00; (100) Fifth Prize $250.00; (2,500) Sixth Prize $10.00; (6,000) **Seventh Prize $12.95 ARV.

   *This presentation offers a Grand Prize of a $1,000,000.00 annuity. Winner will receive $33,333.33 a year for 30 years without interest totalling $1,000,000.00.

   **Seventh Prize: A fully illustrated hardcover book, published by Torstar Corp. Approximate Retail Value of the book is $12.95.

   Entrants may cancel the Reader Service at any time without cost or obligation (see details in Center Insert Card).

5. Extra Bonus! This presentation offers an Extra Bonus Prize valued at $33,000.00 to be awarded in a random drawing from all qualified entries received by March 31, 1992. No purchase necessary to enter or receive a prize. To qualify, see instructions in Center Insert Card. Winner will have the choice of any of the merchandise offered or a $33,000.00 check payable in U.S. funds. All other published rules and regulations apply.

6. This Sweepstakes is being conducted under the supervision of D.L. Blair, Inc. By entering the Sweepstakes, each entrant accepts and agrees to be bound by these rules and the decisions of the judges, which shall be final and binding. Odds of winning the random drawing are dependent upon the number of entries received. Taxes, if any, are the sole responsibility of the winners. Prizes are nontransferable. All entries must be received at the address on the detachable Business Reply Card and must be postmarked no later than 12:00 MIDNIGHT on March 31, 1992. The drawing for all unclaimed Sweepstakes prizes and for the Extra Bonus Prize will take place on May 30, 1992, at 12:00 NOON at the offices of D.L. Blair, Inc., Blair, NE.

7. This offer is open to residents of the U.S., United Kingdom, France and Canada, 18 years or older, except employees and immediate family members of Torstar Corp., its affiliates, subsidiaries and all other agencies, entities and persons connected with the use, marketing or conduct of this Sweepstakes. All Federal, State, Provincial, Municipal and local laws apply. Void wherever prohibited or restricted by law. Any litigation within the Province of Quebec respecting the conduct and awarding of a prize in this publicity contest must be submitted to the Régie des Loteries et Courses du Québec.

8. Winners will be notified by mail and may be required to execute an affidavit of eligibility and release, which must be returned within 14 days after notification or an alternate winner may be selected. Canadian winners will be required to correctly answer an arithmetical, skill-testing question administered by mail, which must be returned within a limited time. Winners consent to the use of their name, photograph and/or likeness for advertising and publicity in conjunction with this and similar promotions without additional compensation.

9. For a list of our major prize winners, send a stamped, self-addressed envelope to: MILLION DOLLAR WINNERS LIST, P.O. Box 4510, Blair, NE 68009. Winners Lists will be supplied after the May 30, 1992 drawing date.

Offer limited to one per household.

THE
CALHOUN WOMEN

BY NORA ROBERTS

If you've enjoyed A MAN FOR AMANDA in the Silhouette Desire line, be sure to look for the rest of THE CALHOUN WOMEN titles in other Silhouette series in the coming months.

August
FOR THE LOVE OF LILAH
Silhouette Special Edition #685

September
SUZANNA'S SURRENDER
Silhouette Intimate Moments #397

Open the door to romance and passion. Sizzling, emotional and compelling—and always a believable and sensuous story—Silhouette Desire books never fail to deliver on the promise of love.

To try other Silhouette Desire titles, please see special savings offer on the back.

CWSD

® Silhouette Books®

SILHOUETTE *Desire*®

30¢   **30¢**

SAVE 30¢
ON YOUR NEXT PURCHASE
OF SILHOUETTE DESIRE®

TO THE DEALER: Harlequin/Silhouette Books will pay 30¢ plus 11¢ handling upon presentation of this coupon by your customer toward the purchase of the product specified above. Any other use constitutes fraud. Proof of sufficient stock (in the previous 90 days) to cover coupon redemption must be presented upon request. Coupon is nonassignable, void if taxed, prohibited or restricted by law. Consumer must pay any governmental taxes. Coupons submitted become the property of Harlequin/Silhouette Books. Reimbursement made only to retail distributor who redeems coupon. LIMIT ONE COUPON PER PURCHASE. VALID ONLY ON SILHOUETTE DESIRE BOOKS IN CANADA.

IN CANADA, MAIL TO:

SILHOUETTE DESIRE BOOKS
P.O. Box 3000
Saint John, New Brunswick
Canada E2L 4L3

Coupons redeemable at retail outlets only.
OFFER EXPIRES DECEMBER 31, 1991.   CWSDCC